Studies of a Provincial Murder

Robert Stewart

Copyright © 2020 Robert Stewart

All rights reserved.

ISBN: 978-1-5272-6707-7

Robert Stewart

The liar

I

It was common to hear a war of words. Arguments occurred frequently and everyone heard them. The couple screamed at each other. The stock prints that hung on the walls in the hallway outside their ground-floor apartment would appear to shake. Even in the basement the noise lost none of its volume. And the clarion call of each argument was often the same question: "So what, you think I am being stupid?"

Lena could not have been surprised to return to the sound of her flesh-tearing friends. Neither could she have been worried; the couple had been together for ten years. Since they had been arguing for as long as anyone could remember, there was a general agreement to allow their wars to rage on unchecked. She found the sound of the couple arguing a comfort. It could lull her into sleep.

The frequent arguments were only the more noticeable of many other noises and sounds. Behind the screams and expletives was a whole orchestra of supporting harmony: the hoarse cough of the central heating kicking into life, and any number of creaks, bangs and whispers. On this night, a particular ticking sound came from somewhere on the fourth floor. It followed a meter that could be heard, only faintly, throughout the whole building. Lena had never heard this sound before; it was quite distinct, though it competed poorly with the couple's hot air.

She had walked through the door, struggling against the whorls of alcohol in her bloodstream and, at some point, crashed into the staircase. Mark and Lucinda's apartment opened onto the hallway. She picked out occasional words: something about a teapot, work and a loser.

The noise, to Lena's ears, sounded mechanical but strangely alive, like a living creature imprisoned in the body of a machine. She had once heard a story about a snake that got trapped in the pipes of a building. The snake had escaped finally via someone's toilet. She imagined snakes swimming through the water pipes of the building. She saw the look on the face of her neighbour, Mrs Garforth, as an irritable black mamba erupted over her carpeted toilet seat and slid across her paisley lino.

If there were black mambas in her water pipes, she wondered how they had got there. She wondered if they could be tamed. Was there a quieter tea-and-biscuits side to the black mamba, misunderstood and overlooked by the wild? Perhaps their owner on the fourth floor had instructed them in good manners and let them roam free in the water pipes. Lena thought this was not very likely. It would be safer to keep the toilet lid down.

The many hours she spent listening to the sound over the next few months led her to believe that it was related in some way to the other sounds in the building. It was like a syncopated counter-rhythm holding together the trilling household. She noticed, after only two weeks, that the ticking started and stopped in almost perfect time with the couple's arguments. A shout would have scarcely left Lucinda's lips before she could hear the familiar tick-ticking. There was, intermittently, an artificial whinny, like the orchestrated sound of the wind in black and white movies.

Lena spent a lot of time thinking about the noise. She could lie on her sofa in her dressing gown, with a tub of chocolate mini rolls resting on her stomach, listening to it. She could bow her head in concentration as she learned about new ways to conquer corns or avoid premature wrinkling as it groused around at the back of her mind.

Lena developed the idea that the noise was an indication of what she called 'Learning'; learning with a capital L. The house was filled with learning; different people and things learning routines and practices. She had, for example, 'learned' a timetable: when she would do her shopping, when she could relax, when she would take a shower. She had also 'learned' the best place to store her groceries, how to organise the furniture. But whenever there was petulance in the air or a slight note of rancour, Lena felt that this was 'learned' from above.

"And that's the sound on the fourth floor," she said.

II

In the winter of 2004, she met Henry in the saloon bar after a Saturday night shift. He wore a grey burlap jumper and jeans; he had folded a leather jacket on the seat next to him. His hair had been clippered recently and he peered down at his glass of beer through frameless spectacles, which, every now and then, he nudged onto the bridge of his nose by screwing up his face. His expression was pensive and gloomy.

Lena had made a habit of talking to strangers in the bar. She was a yapper. If there were an unfamiliar face – particularly someone on their own – she was always curious to know about them. She had talked to walkers passing through the town, couples who were spending a weekend in one of the nearby villages and endless lorry drivers from all parts of Europe who told her about everything from Italian sausages to Bulgarian Banitsa. Contact with strangers kept her in touch with the new and unfamiliar. She liked to learn about the food from different countries. In fact food was her usual point of conversational departure. If someone came from Cornwall she talked clotted cream and pasties; if someone came from Mexico she would start with Guacamole and let the conversation ride. Lena liked to think that food was a universal language that went beyond words. Whether it was bacon in a bun or chicken, cider and cream, where all else failed the stomach would come to the rescue. The stomach was a kind of god. Especially when it rumbled.

She approached Henry out of sympathy. She sauntered across from the bar, her drink in one hand and her duffle coat in the other, happy, if for no other reason than she had finished her evening shift. His personality changed; from a morose beer-sipper, he changed into an outpouring of jokey thoughts and comments. He began to show more interest in his beer, taking large confident gulps that drained his glass. Lena spoke to him liberally and in reply he nodded or moved the conversation along with supportive 'yeah yeah's and short laughs. He would lean back and then forward in his seat. Each moment of their conversation he fidgeted.

Henry had only moved to the town in the last month; he said he spent his time between the North and South; he worked as a journalist for a specialist magazine. He said he travelled widely, at home and abroad as the 'cases' on which he worked required that he follow up every loose end no matter where it might lead. Though he was not senior, he said he had the confidence of the some of his more senior colleagues.

"Did you decide to come north?" asked Lena.

"Well no I … not really. A job came up … I don't know many people here. But I reckon I'm getting to know the place pretty well. This is a regular joint, isn't it? I've noticed a few characters in here."

"There are some weird people in this town."

"Yeah yeah."

"There was a salad chef here … she would tell me off for farting in the kitchen. She said 'Don't gas in the kitchen!' I never gas in the kitchen. I think it was her, but we never drew any conclusive evidence. I think she wanted to divert the blame away from herself, if you see what I mean. As if we would have cared."

"You're the chef here aren't you?"

"Do I smell of halibut?"

"No, no … I have heard about you."

"Really? That's interesting. How did you hear about me?"

"Someone I know."

"Who?"

"Just someone I know."

"Now I'm puzzled. Why don't you want to tell me?"

"I'm quite interested in the river."

"Oh fine …"

Henry laughed.

"Sorry, but I'm sworn to secrecy."

"By who?"

"I have heard quite a bit about you. They say that you boil a pretty decent egg."

"My boiled eggs make quail's eggs look a supermarket snack. I'm a virtuoso egg-boiler."

"There must be a knack."

"No, it's just raw talent."

Henry rotated his pint glass on the table as he looked down at the beer with a faint smile on his face. He seemed to be toying with a thought. Once or twice he looked up as though he was about to speak; he opened his mouth and raised his head, gazing up at the ceiling, like a public orator.

"Someone told me a story about you," said Henry.

"This is another 'someone'. I am getting suspicious of all these 'someone's."

"They said that you once went to a Tupperware party in second hand clothes."

"Yes, I really didn't understand."

"I see."

"I thought it was ... I had never heard of Tupperware. I thought it was an abbreviation for Tuppence Wear or something. I sometimes do things like that. I liked a boy once who was a member of the Free Tibet Campaign, so I joined just to ... you know. When it came to the meetings I had no idea. I thought Tibet was an African politician or something. Then people started talking about Buddhism and the Book of the Dead. It was very confusing. Anyway who is this 'someone'? I think I need to have a few words with them."

"No, no, I don't think you should. Things can be very confusing sometimes. It's sort of reassuring."

"Well what about the river? You said you were interested in the river."

"Can I tell you a story?"

"Okay."

"I was walking down to the abbey the other day. Have you been down there?"

"Yes, of course."

"Well the path goes along the river under the old viaduct, doesn't it? And I walked under the viaduct, and I stopped to look at it when I heard a shout. I turned around and three guys jumped out at me. 'What are you doing?' they asked me. I told them I was just going for a walk. They pointed at some smashed-up brickwork on the underside of the viaduct and said 'You wouldn't have anything to do with that?' I asked them what it was. They said that someone had been sabotaging the viaduct and that they were structural engineers called in to assess the damage. I said I didn't know anything about it. 'Are you looking for the Whistler?' they said. I said I had never heard of the Whistler. They said, 'Well maybe the Whistler's looking for you.' I asked 'Who is the Whistler?' They just laughed.

'Then this midget with a strong Scottish accent and a ginger beard appears. 'Are you the Whistler?' I asked him. The three guys started laughing. I didn't understand what he said exactly, but I think he said the guys were just messing with me and that I should pay no attention. 'Who is the Whistler?' I asked. Now the midget may have said 'They are being cruel' (in fact, I think that's what he did say) but, at the time, I thought he said 'He makes gruel.' I must have looked confused and then thinking that there must be some Scottish connection, I said 'You mean Porridge?' One of the guys said 'Yer what?' I said that I didn't understand. The Scottish guy said 'Ye tryin' te be funny?' I said I wasn't trying to be funny; it was just that I didn't understand.

'One of the guys said 'Sure the Whistler's into oats in a big way.' And then to the Scottish midget he said 'You never know Jock, maybe you're related.' The Scottish guy looked annoyed. He asked me a question. I couldn't understand him properly, but it sounded like he was asking me if there was porridge in his beard. I said 'I can't see any porridge in your beard'. One of the guys said 'Oh not the beard son.' The Scottish guy reared up to me and started swearing. I managed to squeeze in an apology.

'Anyway, this confusion went on for some time. By the end of it all, I thought the Whistler was a Scottish producer of porridge in some way related to the Scottish guy; the guys around me thought I was a tooth-grinning moron with no natural respect for the Scottish diet; and the Scottish guy thought I was a haughty Englishman who looked down his nose at Scotsmen unable to scrape the porridge out of their beard. So, like I say, sometimes things can be confusing. It's good to know that there are other people out there who get confused."

"Who is the Whistler?" asked Lena.

"Well I didn't find out until later. Once we had sorted out our little misunderstanding, the guys offered to buy me a drink at the pub. I asked them about the Whistler. Apparently, one of the guys — he lives in the town — told them all a story about some policeman who lived in the town in 1918. This policeman murdered his wife and dumped the body in the river. Everyone called him the Whistler. He was never caught. Since then two or three people have shown up in the river and some people say it's the Whistler. The other guys were all pulling his leg about it when I walked under the viaduct."

"I hadn't heard that story before. About the policeman and his wife."

"No. Like I say, they reckon it happened in 1918."

III

Lena was content to sit sipping from her large glass of wine. When she was in the company of a large glass of wine she was like a child bribed into silence by sweets or some other luxury. This was even more so at the end of her evening shifts; she liked to relax by leaning back in the warmth of the saloon with her complimentary glass and warm it in the palms of her hand, swilling the deep purple. She would watch the usual crew perched at the bar or come and go through the doors; she would listen to the sedated murmurings from the restaurant tempered by occasional bursts of laughter. In winter especially, she would often fall asleep in this position; her head, weighted and unwilling, would fall slowly against the wooden back of the alcove and her body would crunch rather than curl into the uncomfortable arrangement of available space; a chagrined frown would peep through her curtaining honey-brown hair.

"They are peculiar things rivers," said Henry.

"Yeah? I never thought of them that way."

"I have heard that the river swells very quickly at times. It can burst its banks with hardly any warning. I was told there was a man walking his dog and they were both carried off by the river."

"And what happened to them? Were they eaten by a giant pike?"

"They both drowned. Poor guy. I think he had just gone bankrupt as well! (I guess bad luck comes in waves.) But, I'm telling you they are full of danger.

You wouldn't think it, I know. Most rivers just pass through the countryside unnoticed. They are a sort of pleasant decoration in the landscape; and obviously they aren't like the sea. You swim in the sea – well I suppose it depends where you go – and you can feel the energy of it. There you are, this ... this insignificant creature thrown about by the currents. It could swallow you at any moment. So, I mean people have a respect for the sea because they know it's dangerous. But rivers – they are a different thing. They look so harmless, you see. They look so tranquil. But rivers are deceptive. You shouldn't take anything for granted as far as rivers go. They can be dangerous. How many times have people been caught out by rivers? Yeah? It's kind of complacent."

"I wouldn't know. I don't think a river has ever caught me out."

"Well, it happens. Trust me. And I was thinking about this, and that's what I am saying. This story those guys told me about. This guy…"

"The Whistler."

"It would be easy to take advantage of the river if you wanted to commit a crime like that."

"I wouldn't say easy."

"I've been thinking about this, you know."

"You said that already."

"I got bored one afternoon and so I went down to the river for a walk. I spent some time looking at the river. I think it's possible to predict what the river will do. If you spend long enough looking at it. It's like the intuitive sense of an animal."

"What? Like a fish?"

"It's like there's ... a method."

"A method?"

"Perhaps there's some sort of natural pattern. Perhaps this guy, the Whistler, has control of it."

"Do you spend much time walking by the river?"

Lena envisaged the sad solitary life Henry led as he traipsed his inconsequential frame along the banks of the river each evening engulfed by the rising mist. He would stare at his feet, and, every now and then, look up and sigh like someone bereaved. She wondered if this lonely boat-community boy was really a safe small talker.

"No, no, just sometimes," he said sheepishly.

Then, to Lena's surprise, Henry blanked her. All the life and expression imploded. He gazed into his pint glass. All that remained on the surface was a look of self-examination and sadness indifferent to any who cared to look. It was not dissimilar to the overcast outlook he had weathered when she first set eyes on him. Lena suddenly felt sorry for him.

And then he returned to speak.

"Shall we have another drink? Your glass is empty; would you like another drink?"

"Yes. Thank you."

Henry leaped up.

She looked at him standing at the bar. He shifted weight from one foot to the other. He held a ten pound note in his right hand, waving it eagerly before the eyes of the barman, who dismissed Henry and his waving arm as tawdry and ostentatious. From the side, Henry's face looked flushed and waxy; he was not obviously sweating, but his face looked full, at the threshold of available space.

She was already starting to feel slightly drunk; she looked at his frame; his shoulders were arched slightly but his broader physique was still fairly trim. She took in a deep breath; the familiar taste and smell of alcoholic fumes tickled her senses. She breathed out and slouched into the comfort of her chair. He returned with twinkling eyes and a silly grin slapped across his face. He handed her a large glass of red wine.

"Wow."

"So anyway, did you know," he continued, settling back into his seat with the same grin smothering his face, "did you know that in 1891, Tom Gregory of the then Baker's on St Mary's Street, caught a fledgling white whale in the river, not far south of the sluice gates at Fenton Field?"

"A whale?"

"A white whale. It took eight men altogether to heave it from the water; Tom carried it through the streets on a wooden trailer, like Julius Caesar riding back from Gaul with the spoils of war. There's even a photograph."

"How did it get here?"

"Who knows! As far as I know, the Cald isn't tidal, but I suppose it's possible that it got caught in a particularly strong tidal current and lost its way. Then again, maybe it wasn't from around these parts. Maybe it was a Scandinavian whale. Maybe it came abroad without a phrasebook. There was probably a xenophobic sea bass somewhere near Hull which gave it false directions. Like I say, rivers are full of tricks."

"Sometimes you can see whales off the coast of Scotland."

"They gave it a name."

"Did they?"

"They called it Herb."

"Did they eat it with chips and mushy peas?"

"I don't think that's in the records."

"I have a friend from Scotland. We saw whales up there once. But I just thought they were large rocks. She isn't a small person. And she doesn't have a beard. I find that most Scottish people are quite average-sized."

Lena's thoughts were getting tangled up. She tried to remember everything that Henry had said; she tried to situate her response in the context of their conversation, but she struggled to find the kernel of sense that held everything together. The alcohol was making her tired. She thought she could just eat some chips with mushy peas. She screwed up her face in puzzlement. Her mind started to drift in different directions and she ended up looking at Henry's watch. It was an unusual watch: the hands passed over a small icon of the moon.

"But what do you mean?" she asked eventually, "Why is there a method? I don't understand that … I didn't understand that. Rivers don't have methods. Scientists have methods and teachers have methods; I have a method for batch-cooking guinea fowl. But rivers don't have methods."

"No, but it is a kind of science. That's what I mean. To you or me it might seem arbitrary. To you or me it might seem like we have no control over the river. But if we could understand how the river works we would have an advantage over the people who don't."

"I don't understand how the river works."

"It's like scientists: if a scientist knows how to make a nuclear bomb, it gives them a head start in life. All knowledge is useful in that way. And scientists do understand rivers; they use them to generate hydroelectric power."

"So are you saying that the Whistler is some sort of mad river scientist?"

"Possibly."

"I think you ... how do you know me?" she asked, "Have we met before or something?"

"No. I know you through another source. I know of you through another source, I mean."

"An inside source?"

"You could say that."

"I'm interested to know."

"Naturally."

Things were getting more and more confusing in Lena's mind. It was late. She was tired. Her brain, at the end of the day, was in no fit state to soak up information or perform strenuous calculations. The sniper fire of Henry's conversation shot at her from different directions and she could not hold out. She was starting to think that Henry was an anorak; she could just picture him seated by the river in the rain with a flask of chicken broth and a notepad in which he would jot down subtle variations of water volume and observe the pattern of erosion.

Lena began to wonder what it would be like to date a nerd. Most of her relationships so far had been fished out of a pool of pecs and buns. She imagined Henry standing naked and pale before her in a pair of white underpants half-ashamed of an emerging belly. She pictured the two of them walking through the streets together as he talked about precipitation and iodine concentration. There was some part of her that thought she prized the prospect of a relationship with a nerd highly. In a way, notwithstanding the obvious drawbacks, it would make her feel proud. It would make her feel, if not like an accessory to an acclaimed work of art, then strangely proud of a misshapen defect from the production line: a quiet and sad creature in need of love and care.

He would drag her off from time to time to meetings at a society for the protection of rivers and their wildlife, called something like 'Think Wet' or 'Feel the Flow'. They would attend meetings to discuss the lives of water voles and the changing habits of bull fish. She would meet lots of fleece-wearing, small-eyed river people with thin necks and the eerie comportment of swans, ducks and other riparian creatures. It was strange the way nerds often looked like the object of their obsession. She had once met a man who obsessed over swordfish. It was only after a while that she noticed the unusual length of his conk.

Lena scanned Henry for signs of similarities with rivers; there was nothing striking but the harder she looked, the more she thought she could detect a kind of thin vaporous moisture on the surface of his skin. It was as though his body contained more water than it really needed. This was the clue to their conversation; it was the water talking.

"So," said Lena, thrusting out her chest so that even though she wore a sweater, Henry could get an eyeful, "do you go out much?"

"Why?"

"I just wondered. Personally, I go out with my friends to some places in Leeds. It's not like those girl-parties where you wear nurses' uniforms and devils' horns and have your boobs hanging out," she said, recoiling slightly. "We go to more ... tasteful places. Just where they play good music and you can dance. I like places that are hip but not too energetic."

"Mellow."

"Yes."

"No. No I don't go out much. I don't really know many people here. But I spend a lot of time working on a project of mine. For the magazine."

"What's the project?"

"I am looking for the location of a place in Scotland," he said.

"Is it not on the map?"

"Nope. Or at least it's not on any map that I know about."

"What's it called?"

"*Bas Aberroy*. It's in Perthshire."

"It can't be that hard to find."

"You would be surprised."

"I would be surprised! Is it very small or something?"

"I don't know."

"Is it a town or a village? A hamlet?"

"I don't know. I only have the name."

"What's so special about it?"

"It was a lead thrown my way by a guy in the town. I was doing some research into the history of cryptology; I mean, I have been doing this research for a long time. I discovered a book in the local library. And what the book says – to cut a long story short – is that merchant ships in the South China Sea developed a shipping code based on a map of Great Britain. They used the names of places in Great Britain and the relationship between these places to communicate important pieces of information: you know, anything from basic administrative details and crew names, to reports of piracy.

'But the curious thing is that in the year 1891, several ships in the British merchant fleet went missing: one of the ships had a damaged hull before it set sail, another was a foreign ship that had actually been run by a group of mercenaries before it was commandeered into the fleet, another ship had all kinds of technical problems before it sank, and there were also two ships that set sail together which both disappeared at the same time under the same circumstances. Now, I don't know for sure, because it is in none of the literature, but I think the place *Bas Aberroy* was a location name used in this code to denote something at the time of their sinking. But I am not sure what exactly it was used to refer to. Or if it was used to refer to anything. You see, like I said, the name doesn't figure on any map that I can find. It is not like Manchester or Birmingham or Leeds. Which makes me wonder if it refers to anything at all."

"Wow, it sounds intriguing."

"Yes. The magazine is really keen for me to keep going with this research. That's why I haven't got to know many people since I moved here; I have just been working at it all the time. It's kind of curious."

He laughed.

"I didn't expect to find so much in this town; what with strange shipping codes and stories about murdering policemen, it seems like there are layers of secrecy to the place. But then I am sure all small towns have their skeletons in the closet."

Henry tossed this impression in Lena's direction, so that it might cast his 'research' into the limelight.

"But it was a good reason to come here."

"Most people see the number of pubs as a selling point."

"You see the thing about this sort of information is that it is highly sought after and highly prized. People become very protective of it. Information of this kind has driven men to extreme acts. There are people who want to keep this sort of information secret and who will do anything to keep it secret."

"I *think* I understand."

IV

They walked back through the dimly lit streets; the air was intensely cold; it stabbed at their thin film of protective clothing, discovering and penetrating even the slightest exposure. The night was clear and a layer of ice had started to form on the pavement. It glistened, caught in the blunt lamplight. The streets were silent; there were, unusually for this hour, no shouts or fighting or even muted laughter. A dampened undercurrent of occasional sound came from the nearby motorway, over which there sped cars liberated from the usual logjam of commuters. The shops and other buildings in the high street were equally silent and still. Through the fended-off darkness it was possible to see the white quoins on the corners of many buildings. The silhouette of the brewery stood ahead, towering over the town. Its gates were closed firmly and behind them, blacked out by the night, were the arteries of the brewery: a twisted nexus of pipes, towers, and cables, distilling and steaming.

Henry and Lena graced the pavement with a unique sangfroid; somehow Lena, despite a shorter time spent drinking, was more drunk than Henry. She held onto his arm like an old lady clinging to a supportive railing; even the smallest cracks in the flagstones posed as perilous threats and the small descent to the gutter was a yawning gorge at the bottom of which grinned humiliation and injury.

It turned out that they lived about a mile apart from each other; Henry was renting a house on the north western corner of the town. Since this was loosely on the way to Lena's house, the two walked home together. Their conversation dried up a little to make way for the incidental thrills of the journey home. Were it not for the fact that they were linked at the elbow, both parties would have fallen by the wayside, caught out by one of the obstacles in their way. They carried on in a spirit of teamwork, each supporting the other, so that when a concealed divot or a furtive lamp post or a confrontational gust of wind derailed one member, the other pulled them back on track.

Henry continued to mumble something about the river; he pointed towards the bridge as they left the pub. The pub faced the high street about a hundred yards west of the bridge. They could see lights on the far side of the river and a long row of houses climbing a steady gradient. A combination of lamplight and moonlight skirted off the hump of the bridge.

"Shall we have a look at the river?"

Lena pointed out the temperature.

How long the journey back to Lena's apartment took, neither of them could say exactly. They dragged their sense of time with their heels. The journey as such was a short one (on most days it took Lena no more than five minutes). Her block of flats, a tall four-storey dilapidated town house, was hidden from the main road; it was possible to reach the house by car through a narrow driveway, but her preferred route on foot followed a small network of snickelways that fed into a confined area (Lena called it a 'courtyard' though it was more like a small residential clearing cluttered with dustbins, cats and rats).

Lena thought about Henry only as she reached her doorstep. She was quietly confident that she did not want to sleep with him. She might be persuaded, if he pitched the right note, but, so far, he had given out no obvious signs. She wondered what was passing through his mind. She thought about thrusting her chest at him again, just for fun and to see how or if he reacted; but it seemed inappropriate.

Mark and Lucinda's apartment looked into the small clearing, and they could both hear the stretched voices of the couple.

"What's that?" asked Henry.

"What's what?"

"Those voices shouting at each other. It sounds like someone needs to call social services."

"Oh no. No it's normal. It's the couple … Mark and … it's just the couple … they do this … Mark is a socialist."

"It doesn't sound like a party plenary. It sounds like nuclear war."

"Yes. They know how to shout. They know how to bite each other. They are very noisy."

"Does no-one complain?"

"We don't dare. But anyway, we have to stay in touch. Here, I will give you my telephone number."

Lena reached into her handbag and produced a scrunched-up bit of paper and pen. She leaned inelegantly against the door to the house and scrawled her number as best she could on the piece of paper. She handed the paper to Henry. Henry glanced at it thankfully; and then he looked at it closely. Some kind of recognition crept into his face. He looked wildly at Lena and then, for a reason that Lena was either incapable or just too drunk to explain, he looked upwards, towards the roof of the house.

"Thank you," he replied and recovering his presence of mind, he continued, "that's great; I'll have to stay in touch."

Lena scrutinised him momentarily, while she struggled not to fall over.

"Do you mind if I say something?" she asked thoughtfully.

"No."

"I think it's good to be honest with people. I think it's good to say what you think. I mean if you don't say what you think how can anyone know what you are really thinking?"

Henry looked uncomfortable.

"Sure."

"Well I don't know what it is exactly, I don't know what it is about you but you seem … I have thought this a couple of times this evening … you seem … sad. In some way. I don't know what way."

Henry looked adrift and awkward. His eyes drowned in some kind of all-consuming whirlpool of panic and any trace of a smile vanished from his face.

"How *do* you know me?" she asked hopefully and for the third time.

"Oh, that remains a secret."

She brushed up close to him.

"My door is open to you any time. Just knock."

She kissed him on the cheek and, thrilled by the winded look on his face, she retreated into the house where the sound waves from Mark and Lucinda's argument battered the walls and rebounded in a hollow echo that filled the hallway.

V

Lucinda knocked at Lena's door the following morning. A letter had arrived for Lena the previous day and Lucinda, knowing that Lena checked the mailbox every fortnight at the most, decided to ensure it was delivered safely. She knocked at the door with one hand and clasped the letter tightly in the other. There was no answer. She waited and knocked again. She called out Lena's name. Still there was no answer. She was about to post the letter under the door when she heard stumbling from within.

"Lena?"

Someone or something moved the door handle from the other side. There was a pause.

"There's no key," said Lena's voice.

"What?"

"There's no key ... I can't find the ... I always leave it in the ..."

"Lena, it's Lucinda; I have a letter for you. Are you all right?"

"It was ... Oh hold on, it's here. It's on the floor."

Shuffling movements came from beneath the door. The lock rattled and the door opened.

Lena looked terrible. She was still clothed in her duffle coat and scarf, but they no longer hugged her figure; the coat was twisted half way around her body; some of the buttons had come undone and the crenulated rim was caught on the belt of her jeans. The scarf snaked over her shoulder and down her arm. Her hair, bedraggled and unbrushed, obtruded from her head at unintended angles. She ran her hand through her hair and yawned.

"Hello," she said.

"I have a letter for you, Lena," Lucinda smiled.

The house dated from the late nineteenth century; it had been built originally as an office for the brewery. The brewery vacated the building during the Second World War to make way for the RAF who commandeered it as a regional command centre; there were several, now disused, runways close to the town from where the RAF had flown their bombing missions across the North Sea. There was, hanging on the wall in the main hallway, an old sepia photograph of the administrative staff who had worked there at the time. The brewery had retained formal ownership of the building after the war, but made little use of it, and then sold it in the early nineteen sixties to a local landowner. Since then it had past from one owner to another.

There were three apartments on each of the four floors that comprised the building, except the first, where there were only two. Each apartment, though some were bigger than others, consisted of two rooms and a bathroom. The house, inset from the town houses that overlooked the road, stood among other large serried buildings, built from the same red-brick, in a similar style and to the same dimensions. Light crept in through the windows, but only via the gaps between the surrounding buildings. There was a musty smell that Lena could never quite remove, despite her best efforts.

Because the tenants on each floor were packed together they came to know each other. Lena had known Mark and Lucinda, the squabbling couple from the ground floor, since she had first moved in. Lucinda had become her first real friend in the town. She had introduced Lena to some of her other friends. Between them the couple knew most of the town, or so it seemed to Lena. Mark in particular made it his business to know more than everything reported in the local rag whenever anything of note occurred. Lucinda would often pay Lena visits, in which they would sit down with a cup of tea or coffee and a biscuit and talk. Their conversations billowed and engulfed them; they could run on for hours in spite of themselves.

It interested Lena that Lucinda and Mark had met Henry. They, like Lucinda, had met him in the pub; and like Lena's encounter, he had been sitting on his own for several hours, sipping solemnly through several pints of beer, until Mark had struck up a conversation. They too had learned that he worked as a journalist for a magazine. Mark had said he didn't know of any magazines in the town. Henry, in defence, had explained – a little hastily – that the magazine was not based in the town. He said he commuted to Leeds. Mark had asked the name of the magazine. Henry had stalled before he revealed the name. It was called *Eudaimonia*. It meant 'happiness' in Ancient Greek.

"Mark didn't like him. He called him a phoney."

"I don't know. He seemed kind of harmless. Like a puppy or something."

"Like a puppy?"

"Yeah: sort of puppyish."

Lena finally took off her duffle coat. She did her best to straighten out her hair and look presentable but her efforts were half-baked and unimpressive. She slouched onto the sofa, propped her back against the armrest and wrapped her arms around her pulled-up knees.

"Lena you look ... did you ... you slept in your clothes, didn't you."

Lena nodded her head shamefully.

"You have a habit of talking to strange men."

"Well you talked to him."

"You should be more careful. Did he tell you anything about himself?"

"Like what?"

"I don't know ... just stuff."

"Not really. Just what I said. About being a journalist. He talked about other stuff, but I wasn't paying much attent ... he had a very large chin. Did you notice? It sort of jutted out."

"A shifty chin?"

"I kept trying to picture it in a magazine or something."

"I don't think he's actually *in* the magazine. He writes for it."

"No, I know. But even so."

"Mark doubted he was even in journalism at all"

"Really?"

"He told us some story about a friend who is a stone mason."

"So?"

"He says he does work on the local parish church. He said he works on ...what are they called? Grotesques. That's it. Grotesques. And it's, like ... have you ever been up to the ...? Mark went up there. I wouldn't know a grotesque from a green-eyed monster but there are none on the parish church, I can tell you that much. It was just well ... it was just so much yak. Yak, yak, yak, yak, yak. I don't think he's in journalism. He's probably part of the fishing community."

Lena made a coffee.

It was as she was boiling the kettle that her mind turned to the front door; ordinarily, Lena, more or less without fail, left the key to her apartment in the lock after she had locked the door. But when she had struggled to open it for Lucinda the key had not been in the lock; she had found it on the floor. Even more suspicious, the key had come to rest at the foot of the door ahead of the flattened bristles of the doormat. Now that she thought about it, she had no memory of how she had got from the front door to her apartment, which meant that it was possible someone had helped her up the stairs, left her unconscious on the couch, locked the door behind them and posted the key from the outside. Or she could have just knocked the key out of the lock while drunk.

She was tapping her index finger on the kitchen surface area as she stared at the kettle that had now boiled. Her finger followed a pattern, a steady rhythm like the sound of a grandfather clock. It was quite possible that someone had helped her to the apartment, particularly since she had no memory of climbing the stairs. She could remember leaving Henry on the doorstep and watching him amble, shoulders rounded and arched, down the alleyway into the jet darkness. She could even remember turning and opening the door. Beyond that, there was nothing more than a vague impression of the looming staircase, threateningly steep and high, but nothing close to detail. She looked back at her index finger bouncing up and down on the sheen.

"Have you fallen asleep?!" called out Lucinda.

"No … it's just my finger."

"What? Have you hurt yourself?"

"No … no," she replied.

The upper floors of the building had always interested Lena, mainly because she knew so little about the people who lived on them. She knew a lady from the third floor who worked as a nurse; she had only moved in recently and left under the stairs on the ground floor a collection of cardboard boxes with broken gaffer tape hanging off them. The nurse had met the other people on the third floor. She had mentioned them in conversation. But the fourth floor was remote. Lena had seen weary faces, shuffling up the stairs; she had heard these people speaking, and sometimes, she thought they were speaking a foreign language that sounded a bit like Russian. She envisaged that they all lived together in one stripped-down apartment run by a brusque matriarch with fat hands. She would bustle around the apartment, tidying up scampering children from beneath her feet. Now and then, she would issue reprimands like 'That is enough potato for you, Alexei' or 'You will not beat your brother with pig-iron, Iosif!"

"What are you doing in here?"

"Oh … just smoothing things over."

"We're only drinking coffee. This is not haut cuisine."

Lena shrugged her shoulders and rolled her arms. She had a strange way of curling her arms. It was like a child clutching at a sweet protectively. She folded her fingers into her fist then brought her forearm back over her shoulder. She would often yawn at the same time.

"Did you agree to meet him again?" Lucinda asked.

"Not exactly."

"You're being very secretive about all this. Is something the matter?"

"No. I probably won't see him again," she said stirring the coffee wistfully.

It didn't take much to defeat Lena; she withdrew from the negotiating table with a little less in her portfolio than on her entrance. She ceded territory, clauses, nuances of expression, whole arguments simply because she knew – or she thought she knew – that even if she were in the right, the opposing team would have thought one more thought or spotted one more crucial piece of evidence in their favour.

VI

They drank their coffee together, seated in front of the television.

"Did you ever hear anything about a whale in the Cald?"

"A whale?"

"In the Cald. It was a white whale."

"The river? No. When?"

"Sometime in the nineteenth century. It swam up the river and got caught or something."

"A good catch. Can you eat whale?"

"Of course you can."

"I'm not sure I'd want to. It's not a fish, is it?"

"I eat lots of things that aren't fish."

"You know what I mean."

"So you haven't heard that story before?"

"No."

Lena mused over the contents of an article boasting thirty different culinary uses for Bulgar Wheat. She chewed on mouthfuls of a toasted muffin. The professionalism of her approach to cooking was mirrored in the way she ate her food: she treated the experience ritually, considering each mouthful and each atomic unit of taste with the respect of a primitive killer.

"A boy I knew once told me I was like a scientific principle of entropy."

"He sounds like a real bastard."

"I have a friend," Lena said eventually, "who always – she has never been different – trips over things.

She cannot help it. It is quite funny, really. Wherever she goes, she will always find something to fall over. She has fallen over in the middle of roads, on the top of mountains, in people's houses. She doesn't look where she is going."

"Yeah, it's often like that."

"I am like that with men. I was always like that with men. I have worrying taste. You know uncle Tom who lives in Leeds?"

"Yes I remember."

"He would always tell me I was choosing the wrong man when I was younger. I went for arrogant men, you see. He would always point out to me everything wrong with these men. He would tell me what they did: that they treated women as objects and that they cheated on them. I never listened to him. I quite liked being an object. Sometimes it is easier to be an object. And it ended in tears. At first. So, I am like my falling-over friend. That's how it goes."

"Some people almost *believe* in cruelty."

"I don't know what that means. Things like that go over my head. Cruelty is cruel. Full stop. That's the best of my imagination."

"Yes, I suppose you're right. I wouldn't have said he was cruel. Though I don't know."

"No, but that's what I'm saying. I thought he wasn't."

"He was just weird."

Lena sighed and kicked off her shoes. She pulled off her socks and rubbed her itching feet. She reached over to bookcase on which she had collected an assortment of photographs. Each family member, nearly without exception, looked cheerful. They smiled back at the photographer so effortlessly that it made the snapshot look like jolliness incarnate. They all looked like they could not keep still long enough for the few seconds it took to capture the moment. The only exception was uncle Tomas, notable for his extreme contrast with the others. He was, in the photograph, a man in middle age with short brown hair, gimlet eyes and a high forehead. He looked stern. Alongside the other photos he also looked irritated; he was the only serious member of the family – a successful lawyer or banker perhaps – who had no time for amateurish clowning across the branches of the family tree. But if the photo were abstracted from the others, it gave the impression that he was thinking about his pose, as though the furrowed brow and pinched eyes were planned for the photograph.

"Pinocchio ended up inside a whale, didn't he?" Lena said carelessly.

"He got out in the end."

"Still, it can't have been much fun while it lasted."

"No."

"I remember that story not because I was frightened I would end up in a whale but because I was frightened of dogs. When I was young, I thought they would eat me. I got so worried that I began to write stories about it. I had a little notebook and I would hide in my room, imagining what life would be like from the inside of a dog's stomach."

"Pretty disgusting, I would have thought."

"I wanted to convince myself that life inside a dog would not be that bad. I knew it wouldn't be good, but I just had to make the best of a bad job. Did you ever do anything like that?"

"No."

"In the end, it became a sort of safe place. A place to go and imagine things. Like children do. I am friends with a paediatrician. I once told him about my imaginary life inside a dog. He looked very disturbed and so I asked him what it meant. I asked him if there was a footnote in Sigmund Freud about me. He said there wasn't. He told me I was just nuts."

Lena began to talk about dogs, about the scores of dogs she had known, the black-faced border-collie her family had kept and its antics; she talked about a dog school organised and run by a friend of her grandparents, the community of dogs that she encountered on a daily basis: a gentle, Friesian Saarloos Wolfdog, a toothy Great Dane, a meat-headed Rottweiler, gums caked in a treacle slather, and a dock-tailed Doberman pinscher with an effete interest in lavender. Her mind strolled curiously around incidents, anecdotes and breeds in a dilettantish way, half of her there in name only. She squandered the facts and figures as though there was a hoard of data available to her.

She read the letter Lucinda had delivered. The letter was one of many from her father. Lena's father had a phobia of phones; he avoided using phones except when it was absolutely necessary. The reasons were not clear. If and when he were ever asked about it – which he seldom was – he stumbled over his thoughts and they clogged somewhere between his brain and his mouth.

"I don't know ... it's well – how should I put it? ... it's ... they trouble me. They are attached and I am unattached ... they trouble me. Yes."

For whatever reason, he chose to write when he wished to contact anyone and this he would do either by email or by letter, though his preference was by letter. He enjoyed the act of crafting a letter; he would spend a solid hour scribbling in notepads before he reached for his fountain pen and his store of embossed letter-headed paper, printed by a backstreet printers seven years previously and which he had still not exhausted. In this case, he had written to tell Lena that he was planning to visit her in the following week. He would be passing through on his way to a meeting with one of the country's foremost bicycle manufacturers (Lena's father was a regular contributor to a magazine for cycling enthusiasts called 'Work that Chain!'). He scrawled facts, figures and a small schematic diagram onto an attached piece of paper. Lena stared at the drawing, looking at phrases like 'subseatstay compression struts', her mind half-focused. Her father's energy was draining. She could not be sure what to expect. All his visits were an adventure, but they also made her nervous.

"I think these days I am turning into a winowoman," Lena said, rubbing her head. "This is what happens when you work in a restaurant. They offer you free drinks."

"It's a celebrity lifestyle. You could always say no."

"There are a lot of things jumbling around inside my head at the moment," she said prodding her forehead with her finger.

Henry was niggling at her brain, returning, again and again as though her damaged memory were trying to tell her something.

"Do you really think he was lying? Why would he lie to me? I didn't know him. I don't understand. Do you think he is weird? Do you think he was lying?"

VII

She discovered, in the days and weeks that followed, that Henry had fed them all a medieval banquet of lies. Solid evidence came through when she took a walk down to the viaduct. She walked under the viaduct to look for the signs of damage Henry had referred to in his story. There was none. The same nineteenth century brickwork was still in place smoothed over with a thick layer of grey dirt and cobwebs. She even asked Mark if he knew if the viaduct had undergone any repairs. Mark asked around at the council but no-one knew anything about it.

She walked through the high street trying to digest Henry's lie. The street was relatively quiet; a few pedestrians ambled along the pavements, though with no interest in any of the shops, which were all closed. The tearooms on Spa Street were, as usual, busy with the predictable clientele: walkers exploring one of the many walks along the river and weekend visitors to the town, families finding fun down by the river; old ladies at weekly get-togethers. She walked around the streets slowly, half-looking at the facades of the different shops. She walked by the delicatessen, by *Brown and Sons* hardware store and *The Big Noodle* Chinese restaurant. On the opposite side of the road was the bank, and, adjacent to it, the chippy-cum-hog roast that only ever opened on a Friday and Saturday night. She could see the entrance to the old brewery ahead. Above the door was a crescent-shaped fanlight.

She retraced the journey she had taken with Henry, looking for clues that they might have left accidentally on the pavement. She walked to the bridge. She leaned over to look at the river. The river at this point was very shallow all the way across; even from the bridge it was possible to see the riverbed. Often, though not so often in winter, fishermen waded into the river and stood for hours at a time, like huge lubberly herons balancing on the uneven rocky floor. There was a story, or a myth, about a fisherman who caught weil's disease when he accidentally slipped up in the water; most versions of the story focused on the speed at which it took him to die.

To her right, as she looked down stream, Lena could see the bus station. Standing outside the shelter was a collection of tracksuits, smoking anything they could inhale. The tracksuits owned the bus station. They marked their territory with cider bottles, cigarette butts and used condoms; some came from the sprawling council estate behind the bus station and others (the money) came from the dolly housing estates, the ne'er-do-well sons and daughters of local businessmen.

Mist crept up around the town. It made it hard to see much beyond the viaduct half a mile downstream. Recipes swirled around her head. In place of buildings she saw meats, casseroles, and platters. She had always wanted to create a recipe associated with a place; she had tried to think of something appropriate for the town. Standing in her way were any number of Sunday roasts, Toad in the Holes, Suckling Pigs and Steak and Ale pies; these simple recipes had cornered the market. They reached back into the distant past of the region as though metaphysically essential to the very nature of things. She looked at the river and thought about white whales.

No-one she asked knew of a man who had been swept away by the river or about the discovery of a white whale in the nineteenth century. Neither had any of her friends ever seen a Scottish midget or heard a story about a policeman who murdered his wife. They were also now sure that there was no magazine based in Leeds called *Eudaimonia*. And if Henry had lied about all this, there was no reason to suppose he had not lied about everything else.

Some of the bar staff and kitchen staff fuelled her irritation by asking about her Saturday night with Henry, but she tried to dismiss it with a shrug of the shoulders. She had, after two weeks, more or less dismissed the events of that night from her memory, until she saw his chin protruding from a column on the fifth page of the local newspaper as she finished her usual cup of coffee in *The Dirty Café* on Eustace-Janeway Street.

He appeared in the newspaper under the headline 'Missing Post Office Manager'. The article didn't seem to know for how long he had been missing. One neighbour said "There was nothing untoward when I last fetched eyes upon him. He was his usual self. He was full of tricks and teases. I would have said he was as happy as Larry." His family had phoned his home – a weather-boarded bungalow on the north western edge of the town – but received no answer.

It was only when they phoned his work that they started to really worry because he had not checked in for two weeks. His father had driven up to visit the bungalow. It was reported that he was not known to have gone missing before. The article urged anyone with any news or knowledge to contact the police.

Lena was confused, at first, by the article because it referred to Henry by a different name; it called him Andrew McInnis. It stated that he had moved to the region only recently from Nottingham after he had secured a position as a junior manager with the Post Office. It made her wonder if the article was about someone else who only looked like Henry; but his face was unmistakable. If it were someone else, it would have to be his double and she found that equally hard to believe. There seemed to be a recurrent plea for information running throughout the article. One of his work colleagues described him as withdrawn and quiet. Nowhere did the article make it explicit, but it suggested that neither his family, nor his work, nor the police had much information about him.

Lena went to visit the police. She told them the story of her night out with Henry. She told them some of the things he had told her: about the river, the murder, the policeman, the place in Scotland.

The police noted everything down, but received this evidence and her testimony not with the frenetic sense of purpose she hoped it might elicit, but with a phlegmatic and slightly dull worldly wisdom born of respect for protocol and rigour. Lena even had the impression that the police had heard similar things from other sources, though they were too discreet (or possibly disinterested) to say this openly.

She did hear one of the officers mutter "Sounds like a tall tale," when she told them about the policemen, but mainly they seemed more interested in offering her cups of tea.

Lena thought there might be an opening for someone with more knowledge of hot beverages in the police force, and was just musing on how one might use jasmine or camomile tea for interrogation purposes, when an abruptly spoken police officer ushered her back into the street.

The town only showed a passing interest in the story; the local press ran just the one article. Even the household's interest lessened with the lack of any news to sustain it.

VIII

Routine and the events of each day flushed the memory of Henry out of her system. Thoughts came at her left right and centre. She struggled enough to remember what shifts she was working throughout the week, what fresh food she would need to buy at the crack of dawn and what she had to do in the time left available to her.

She enjoyed her early morning purchases; she enjoyed buying fish in particular. The fishmonger was run by two brothers: Barney and Wiltord. They purchased their fish fresh off the boat. They took it in turns to make the drive there and back to the coast each morning. They seemed to have some sort of arrangement with one fisherman, who had a vast collection of ice-age bones he bragged about. Lena imagined the North Sea fishing community holding annual competitions to see who had dragged up the largest number of ice-age bones:

"Fetched up new bit o' mammoth this mornin'!" said one voice in her head.

"Oh aye!" said another. "Were it the middle or late Pleistocene?"

The brothers would always refer to each other directly by their first name and they usually had a story to relate. Wiltord had a 'missus' with a foot problem. She had 'fat ankles' and had to wear some sort of supportive footwear. On holiday at a farm in Scotland, she had once got her foot stuck in a bucket of chicken feed and limped around the farmyard chased by hungry chickens pecking at her swelling.

Lena had a talent for pottering, for meandering down the high street with her mind fixed upon the displays and shop fronts. She enjoyed talking with the butcher about meat; she liked to know his opinion of all the different cuts. She would lean against his counter as he served other customers, and talk lamb shanks and shin beef. She enjoyed examining the cheeses and delicacies, the krakowska sausage and large Mediterranean butter beans in the delicatessen. She enjoyed chatting to people in the street. She had come to know a number of old ladies, some of whom raced each other down the high-street in their motorised wheelchairs.

There was nothing too ordered or planned in the way Lena went about things; she could drift into her apartment to find that she had spent an hour longer shopping or drinking a coffee than she had planned and she now had only five minutes to get changed and arrive on time for work. If she were to step-stone back through the events that comprised her average day, she could find no broader theme. Her mind was a butterfly mind that fluttered between unrelated desiderata: a wine auction, a colour pantone, a long untroubled morning, a new implement for peeling potatoes.

Periodic shocks and jolts interrupted her routine; and they usually stirred her into a whirl of panic. She would be sitting trouble-free, as she read a book or talked to one of her friends, when something would flick a switch in her memory and she would remember something else important. She would stand up and flap.

The more Henry and his disappearance receded into the past, the less frequently it happened, but, from time to time, her memory would dredge him up. It seemed to her, in these rare moments of reflection, that her memory was a finite space subjected to constant invasions, which cut to size all her existing memories. This meant that she was no good for anything. She could not be relied on as an accurate store of information. She was like an old piece of technology that served no useful purpose. She was a piece of nostalgia. No doubt, at some point in the future, she could find employment touring with an entertainment troupe. The leader of the troupe would find her some act to perform and audiences would clap and laugh, shouting 'How marvellous! How Quaint!' She was the next dog on wheels, she thought.

Sometimes it bothered her. When it mattered, it bothered her.

She kept thinking about the key. She thought about it over and over. She never forgot to leave the key in the lock, no matter how drunk. It was not even something she thought about. She had trained her body to do it, so that she had no need to rely on her memory. If it had not fallen from the lock, it could only mean that someone had posted the key under the door. In which case, she wanted to know who.

She worked her memory hard at these times; and the more she unveiled the line between her memory and her forgetfulness, the more frustrated she became.

Just walking up the stairs from the door could feel eerie. Retracing the steps she must have taken always made her think about the gap in her memory. She felt that the missing details were hidden or concealed somewhere in the space between the front door and her apartment. Each time she ascended the stairs she looked around nervously, at the walls and down at the hallway beneath, expecting to find signs or clues. It was as though the missing details had become an invisible person whose presence was clear enough, but who remained unknown.

IX

Sometimes – usually when she had been drinking – she would peer through the spy hole in her front door at the landing and the top of the stairs to see if she noticed anything untoward. It was around this time that she began to take real notice of the sound somewhere on one of the floors above. She caught herself one evening tapping her fingers in time to it. This was the first time she had acknowledged it properly. She could not quite locate it and so she wandered around the rooms of her apartment trying to pin it down. Shouts from Mark and Lucinda's apartment attacked her from below. She peered through the spy hole of her door. The corridor was empty.

Lena had never visited the fourth floor. She opened her front door and walked out into the hallway. The noise was slightly louder from there as was the noise of her friends below. The hallway was still, only suggestive of the sounds in each apartment.

She followed the ticking sound to the third floor. Televisions could be heard from inside some apartments, but still the sound seemed to be above her. The corridors on the building became more Spartan as she climbed and the carpet recovered some of its colour. The walls on the fourth floor had not been painted for many years; there were large patches where the paintwork had come away as well as scratches and illegible graffiti. She could see that there were four apartments on the fourth floor. The staircase led to a corridor shorter than any of the corridors on the other floors; there were three doors on the left of the corridor and one at its end. An enormous single-paned window brought in light; through it she could see gable ends and the tops of adjacent buildings. The noise came from the apartment at the end of the corridor.

By now she could hear little of the other sounds in the building; Mark and Lucinda had faded out completely and, as if to suggest that the people on the fourth floor lived in the kind of squalor she imagined, she could not even hear the water pipes. No sound came from the two apartments to the left of the corridor, and none of the doors had a number. Instead they had names: the first apartment on her left was called 'Omicron' the second, 'Nu', the third 'Upsilon' and the apartment at the end of the corridor was called 'Sigma'. She approached Sigma and pressed her ear up to the door slowly.

She could hear the ticking noise, louder, constant and unmoving, somewhere deep in the belly of the apartment. She willed the noise to move, to come closer, to give some indication that someone had created it or turned it on. She was trying to make out the sound in more detail, when she thought she heard a shuffle very close to her on the opposite side of the door. She glanced down at the foot of the door, searching for some evidence of movement. Close on the tail of the shuffling movement, there erupted into her right ear a hoarse cough, projected at her from only the width of the door. She gasped, stumbled backwards, fell onto the carpet in panic, scrambled to her feet, turned and ran.

She didn't stop to look back; in her mind, the door was opening as she hurried along the corridor and down the stairwell. There would be no lights on in apartment Sigma and out of the darkness, at the foot of the door, a large boot would appear. It would be a boot that belonged to a hairy Russian, wearing a thick overcoat over a vest. He would have a beard, a shashka and a scowl. Or if not, it would be something much worse. She ran into her apartment and locked the door behind her.

She grabbed her phone and kept watch, peeping through the spy hole in the door. She shuffled about on her feet. She peered out at the empty corridor for about five minutes, before she noticed that she was standing on a bit of paper. It had crumpled underneath her feet. She bent down and picked it up. It was a small scrap of notepaper folded in half. A single sentence had been scribbled at the head of the paper. It read:

> *Do you know what they say about the bird that dived into the water?*

In the days that followed, she left the piece of paper on the mantelpiece where she could see it. She would look at it warily from time to time, as if she expected it to do something mischievous. She examined it carefully. She fondled it and smelled it. She looked closely at the handwriting, but it was unfamiliar. It was messy, barely legible. It was the product of an unpractised hand; there were no frills or shapely curlicues. Once she was satisfied that the letter posed no threat and that it was not about to uproot and disappear into the dusty clutter of her apartment, she locked it inside a drawer in her bedroom. Each morning, as she returned from the shower, she checked the drawer to ensure the letter was still there.

She continued spying on the corridor from time to time, particularly in the early evening when the tenants were returning from work. She would leap to her feet and approach the door as soon as she heard the sound of footsteps or voices on the staircase. She saw many people, most of whom she had seen before. There were only two faces that she didn't recognise. These two, she decided, were the inhabitants of the fourth floor and one of them lived in apartment Sigma. This meant that, unless a terminal convalescent or someone who, for whatever reason, chose to hide away, also lived in the apartment, one of these two was the person who had coughed loudly in her ear.

There was a man and a woman. It was possible that either of the two characters lived in apartment Sigma. They both, despite their physical differences, dovetailed with her imagination. They were both, in their own way, seedy and secretive. The woman was young, blonde and petite with pallid, waxy skin and dark eyes that intimated some kind of trouble or substance abuse. If Lena looked closely, she could see a glaze over the surface of her eyes. It made her look tearful. It was unlikely, though, that the woman lived in apartment Sigma. The cough had not sounded like the cough of a woman; it was too thunderous and throaty, too smoked-out and black. The man was quite different: he was abnormally fat. He bouldered up and down the corridor with a borrowed swagger, crushing everything in his way: cobwebs, small animals, petite women. It was difficult to know what he was thinking as he moved, because his round face concealed his expression. It made him look dour and stubbornly silent, as though he might burst into a rage at the slightest provocation. His hair was long, tangled and sweaty; he often carried a newspaper under his arm and a white plastic bag from the local newsagents in one hand.

She was sure, for several days after her journey to the fourth floor, that she would see some sort of repercussion; but each day she looked out of her spy hole at the same people going about the same routine. So she ostriched the event. She found things to keep her entertained and preoccupied. She would, for example, stare at the mounting pile of papers and magazines she had accumulated in the corner of her room and think of uses for them or ways to clear them from the space they occupied. She could spend an afternoon looking through each one for every example of the word 'botox', 'is' and 'bad' and glue the clippings onto an old vest. She also found distraction in more simple activities, like ironing.

But mostly, if she had returned from a shift or even if she had spent her afternoon and evening out with some friends, she found the courage to sleep off her concerns about the sounds and symptoms of misbehaviour that lived elsewhere in the apartment building.

Robert Stewart

The button box

I

Tomas had only lived in Leeds for the past two years. In that time, Lena had seen him four times. He ran an educational theatre programme at the West Yorkshire Playhouse and taught theatre and performance part-time at a private school to the north west of the city. Fifteen years ago he had been an out-of-work actor who landed minor roles in West End productions and the occasional lead role in a repertory show. He had appeared as an extra in television soaps and played an embezzling trust fund manager in a crime series called *Donovan's Dirt*. He had also taken part in a tour of Euripides' *Medea* that ran throughout eastern Europe and into Greece. He had enjoyed this, he said, more than anything else he had done, and, for a time after the tour had ended, he travelled throughout Europe as a street performer. He learned the basics of the *Commedia dell' Arte*, in which he always played Harlequin.

Opportunities dried up as time went by, and Tomas drifted into theatre administration, and then the crossover between theatre and education. He had done many other jobs: he had worked as a bricklayer, a cab driver, a clerk for the Inland Revenue, and as a hand on a farm.

The two brothers had grown up in a small village in the North York Moors. Their father had been an evacuee from Leeds who had stayed in touch with his adoptive family and then married the eldest daughter. He had taken a job teaching French and German at a school in Scarborough, where he eventually became the headmaster. He believed emphatically in education. Children, he drummed into his own, should be exposed to the history and fruits of many disciplines from an early age. He believed this not because it enabled them to get a good job or raise their standard of living; he thought learning was *desirable*. Without education – without an education that could draw out the natural magnetism of learning – children would suffer and society would suffer.

The only other thing he believed in was God, passionately and unequivocally. He became a lay preacher at a local non-conformist church and insisted that his children attend Sunday school and learn large chunks of the Bible off by rote. And he insisted that they discover its meaning.

The brothers chafed against each other as they grew up. The most they had in common for a long time was that they were both young. They laughed at the strange accent of their grandfather and his colloquialisms. They made up adventures in the hay barn and carved out intricate tunnels through the long sedges and tussocks of summer meadows. They worked together on elaborate strategies to outwit geese.

The older they became the more they discovered that this was only a passing similarity: John's interests were measured and developed. Tomas' development and interests were more fitful: for long periods of time it appeared that he had no interest; he sulked. But he would go through phases of fanatical interest: when he was first exposed to the periodic table he learned it by heart in an evening and would reel it off proudly from memory before members of his family. He also shared his father's obsession with religion; Sunday school was one of the few occasions in the week that captured his full attention. He enjoyed practising his handwriting by copying chapter and verse from the New Testament. And he would write his parents letters proclaiming his 'ardent and soulful evangelism'.

The history of the two brothers was a history of gradual separation: John went to university; Tomas travelled to London and got a job working in a shop that sold dirty books; John married and had a family; Tomas remained single; John had only travelled once (to the Netherlands where he met his wife); Tomas had walked and hitchhiked through most of Europe, parts of America, north and south, and India, roughing it in low-budget accommodation or simply sleeping in ditches; John worried about the well-being of his family; Tomas spent a year and a half living in an unheated boat on the river Thames, where he drank whisky in order to sleep. The only thing they both had in common was their loyalty to their family and, while the family was still alive, it provided the only reason for the two brothers to see each other at all.

The times they had arranged to meet independently of the family were few and far between, though they had, since the death of their father, kept in close contact with each other. Most of the occasions they met were awkward in one way or another. John had noticed that Tomas had become progressively more prickly and unpredictable; the slightest change of mood or comment could receive a barbed response.

II

John Jennings, or Papa J as he preferred not to be known, arrived at eight thirty, an hour later than he had planned. He said he had been caught in traffic. There had been an accident on the motorway near Huddersfield. He brushed the rain from his coat, muttered something about poor parking facilities and walked into the living room where he shook Tomas by the hand. He was awkward, even nervous, greeting his brother.

"Birds!" he said eventually. "I heard the other day that there is an environmentally friendly firm of lawyers in Manchester who have started using carrier pigeons rather than the Royal Mail. They have a department in the firm called 'Pigeons and Alternative Communication'. That's a good one, in my view. There are too many cars on the road these days and not enough pigeons in the sky."

"Is that right? Are they environmental lawyers?" said Tomas.

"No, they are a firm of commercial lawyers, making headway in the top 100 law firms in the country. I think it will mark the beginning of a trend. Soon, all over London, you won't find the scores of red and yellow mail vans, but the sky will be packed with carrier pigeons carrying legal documentation! Oh yes!"

"That will cause a bit of a flap," said Tomas.

"That's rubbish!" said Lena. "You've just made that up, haven't you?"

"Well ... ah ha! But it's a neat principle. And then there are migratory birds to consider."

Tomas looked around at the disordered state of Lena's apartment with the suggestion of a smile on his face. He seemed to be looking for a quizzical comment.

"I like the clever use of boxes in the room, Lena. And is that a pair of socks? Oh yes it is."

"Shut up. I'm the queen of taste. I have six A-levels and a PhD in good taste. I'm the headline act at the theatre of style and seduction."

"Is that a box of sanitary towels I can see behind the sofa?"

"You two can't talk!"

"Style and taste require affluence and culture. We were hindered from childhood: we grew up in Yorkshire. Our idea of culture was a performing field mouse called Tweed. Entertainment for us was the button box."

"Of course ... oh yes, the button box. I had nearly forgotten."

"How could you forget the button box? It was integral to our lives. It taught us basic economics."

"What was the button box?" asked Lena.

"What does it sound like? It was a box full of buttons," said Tomas.

"Oh but it was more than that. The box went back ... it was in the family. It went back ... it went back to the nineteenth century. It was a huge great big clunking oak chest that we wheeled out on Sunday afternoons when we were bored."

"What for?" Lena asked.

"For anything. There was ... there was something ... very basic ..."

"There was an appealing simplicity about it," interrupted Tomas. "It is hard to imagine just how far a collection of buttons could keep a pair of young boys entertained. Part of the attraction was the box itself and part of the attraction was the buttons. The box had been hand-crafted by our great-great-great grandfather, who was an employee of the Broadacres in York. To us it was so vast and so intricately made, that it was possible to spend most of an afternoon just emptying it of all its contents."

"That was one of the main games we played," continued John. "We would always ignore the buttons at first because ... yes, because we were so keen to clear it all out."

"Because, you see," picked up Tomas, "our great-great-great grandfather had thought about his creation. It was no ordinary box he had knocked out one Sunday afternoon in his workshop. He spent time thinking about it and planning it; there were, of course – and he knew this from the beginning – the standard compartments in the box: large spaces that even the clumsy and cack-handed could access. But this was a trick, you see. He created these compartments to be obvious and generations of men and women filled these compartments with buttons of all kinds. And the clumsy and cack-handed would shovel in their mitts and withdraw sums of button! But they didn't find the real treasure. And we knew better than the clumsy and cack-handed. We had little mitts, the hands of children and the wit and curiosity of children.

'Our great-great-great grandfather had worked into his creation small niches and drawers, some more obvious than others. The more canny members of our family had, over the generations, concealed prized objects and special buttons. It was, for example, rumoured that our grandmother kept a button from the tunic of her husband's army uniform after she learned of his death in the First World War. But the key thing is that our great-great-great grandfather – Grandfather Henry Dickson – made it as difficult as he possibly could to find these compartments. He devoted so much of his spare time to what was, in effect, a puzzle. So, as I am sure you can understand, our first task was to remove all the buttons in order to find the concealed compartments.

'There was even a rumour that Grandfather Henry Dickson had created a small network of tunnels and trap-doors triggered by weights. This meant that whenever someone put something into the box or took something out, some buttons would change compartment; so, even if you found one of the small compartments he had crafted, there would be no guarantee that any object in it would remain there."

John looked at Lena to gauge the look on her face.

"Then why would anyone put anything in it?" she asked.

"It's a good question. But, by the same logic, why would anyone create it in the first place? What purpose did it serve? To entertain? There is a word to describe the button box: hermetic."

"Hermetic," repeated Lena, sounding the syllables.

"But come on," said John, "I mean … it's … let's not go too far. Mother was always fishing in and out of it for buttons. It had a practical purpose. And you have … what about the buttons? We would often just … never mind the box … we would count the buttons and barter with them. We would … do you remember? We would look for all the ones that were the same and arrange them. We would spread them all out on the table. Do you remember the table? It was … how old was it?"

"It was a Victorian pine farmhouse table."

"Did you ever find all the compartments?"

"We found some, but the problem was that no-one knew exactly how many compartments there were. Grandfather Henry Dickson never left a blueprint. I was more concerned to find all the compartments than your father. You have never been interested in that kind of thing, have you John? Not really interested?"

"Tomas would get quite agitated."

"I once nearly smashed the box with a hammer to see its inner mechanics with my own eyes. But mother said it would be cheating."

"And you became churlish about it. You sulked and refused to play with it again."

"Yes, but that was only because I wanted to see how it worked and, all credit to him, because

Grandfather Henry Dickson had outwitted me. I hated him for a time. I went around swearing at him. I remember telling myself I would invent something far better, like an aeroplane. And even now, I think, if he had that much talent why didn't he invent an aeroplane or a computer or a nuclear bomb? Anything but a fucking button box!"

"What happened to the button box?"

"I have it," said John, "in my loft; I took it with a whole bunch of other stuff when mother died."

"Does that mean I will inherit it at some point?"

"Yes, I suppose so. Well, you can have it now, if you want."

"Did you ever think of having it analysed."

"By a button box analyst?" Tomas asked.

"By a carpenter or something. It might be one of its kind."

"It is one of its kind," said Tomas. "It would confound any garden variety carpenter."

"How do you know? You're not a carpenter."

"Tomas is right," said John. "Even the most skilled carpenter would have trouble with it. On the continent they have specialist carpentry schools; if you took it to France, you might just find someone. There is probably someone in a room at the top of a tower in Gascony — we'll call him Philippe — who spends his days shaping barley twist table legs."

"But Philippe uses the metric system," objected Lena. "Anyway, I bet there's a completely different tradition of carpentry in France. Look at their furniture; it's all ... artistic and gilded."

"Yes, but I am not talking about French aristocrats. I am talking about Jean-Pierre Ordinaire, Mr *Vin de Table*. The French working man has plain-wood furniture. He is a simple creature. He uses simple well-crafted wood for his tables and chairs. You don't want rococo when you're scoffing down Camembert with a hunk of French stick. You have to think rustic. And that's what makes a tradition; a skilled tradition."

"What do you know about French carpentry? You don't know anything about it. Anyway if Jean-Pierre Ordinaire can only make simple tables and chairs, he would stand no chance …"

"Ah, but simplicity can be deceptive … you've only got to look at the simplest of sentences – 'The cat sat on the mat', for example – to know that it takes considerable skill to arrange …"

"A five year-old can do it. What do you mean?"

"Philippe is no simpleton; he has several degrees and several apprenticeships working on gothic cathedrals. He has studied under the most illustrious carpenters … and he has performed calculations and shaped wood in ways that only the most learned know how. I am convinced that he could account for the button box easily. He could do it before breakfast with the smell of *pain au chocolat* wafting through the …"

"But Philippe is a ploughman's lunch! He is a simpleton! Anyway what's so complicated about a table leg?"

"If you examine a table leg, you will notice that they are far more intricate than you would have imagined. There are very precise incisions ... exact calculations that require ... incidentally Philippe would never eat a ploughman's lunch. I think we are talking more of a country spread: *pâté de campagne*, mushrooms, bread and a bottle of plonk."

"Philippe is ... you said he is a simpleton. He is Jean-Pierre Ordinaire. He couldn't do the job!"

"I think you'll find Philippe pleasantly surprising."

"I think Philippe is simple."

"Well we are talking about Philippe King of the Carpenters, a man with 3 PhDs in Carpentry, who specialises in the knotty problems of wood and spends his weekends solving spatial problems for fun. My money is on Philippe."

"Now you're just being silly, Papa J."

"Don't call me Papa J; it gives the ... it makes me sound like a hoodlum."

III

Throughout the meal that followed Tomas turned quiet. He shovelled in mouthfuls of his meal and chewed thoughtfully on chunks of meat. He overshadowed the conversation from an observational distance. He raised his eyebrows in response to some comments and frowned at others. Otherwise he wore his expression like a clunky coat of armour. He had not withdrawn from the conversation; he looked busy, despite his silence, as though he might pass comment at any moment.

John went to the kitchen to look for a bottle opener. Tomas continued to chew through a piece of meat. He smiled at Lena.

"This is excellent – excellent cooking."

"Thanks."

"Your apartment's kind of pokey isn't it?" he said, once he had finished chewing. "It feels slightly claustrophobic with three people in it. It's almost like we are eating in your bedroom."

"Yeah, I guess."

"Mine's not much different."

He paused and took a sip from his glass of wine. He began to pick strands of masticated lamb out from the gaps between his teeth. Lena barely noticed at first, but he seemed to be making a show of it. He stretched his mouth to full capacity and poked around inside it with his index finger so that Lena could see the grey glimmer of his fillings.

"Tom! I don't want to see your tonsils."

Tomas retrieved his finger and closed his mouth without saying anything. He wrapped his knuckles on the table as he stared at the remaining contents of his plate. Lena smiled politely.

"Did you get my note?" he asked eventually.

Lena replied through an incipient awakening.

"What note?"

"I sent you a note."

"By mail?"

"No: hand-delivered."

"You came here?"

"I sent an emissary."

"What did it say?"

Tomas looked at her closely.

"*Do you know what they say about the bird that dived into the water?*"

"You sent it?"

"Yes. Did you not get it?"

"Yes, I got it. Yes. When did you send it?"

"A fortnight ago; about then."

"You left it under my door."

"That was my instruction."

Questions filled Lena's mind; there were so many angles from which she might appraise this new piece of information. She was sure from the moment he had mentioned the note that it was significant in some way, but she could not see how exactly. The way Tomas had mentioned it – coolly and incidentally – suggested that he thought nothing of it; he had said it as though it was something to mention in passing as they waited to return to serious business: the mystery of the button box. Though in Lena's mind, everything was upside down; the note was, for her, the thing that mattered, and the button box was the trivia.

"What *do* they say about the bird that dived into the water?" she asked.

John returned, waving an opened bottle of wine.

"Alcohol," said Tomas, registering the appearance of the bottle like the victim of terrible brain disease reduced to the expression of single words. The word seemed to soak into his bloodstream before it gave rise to a complete thought. "Alcohol, like anything, can be both a good thing and a bad thing. The key, they say, is to enjoy it in moderation. But you only have to dodge the vomit-hurling throughout the central thoroughfares of British provincial cities to see that it is not enjoyed in moderation. It burrows deep and takes its poundage."

"Don't worry, I'll hurl my vomit privately," said John with the bottle poised over his glass.

"The point is that alcohol is something in which people take enormous pleasure but which is also destructive. Some people drink knowing the harm it does them. Some people even drink in order to inflict self-harm."

"Do you want a glass or not?" asked John, holding up the bottle.

"Yes. I am not objecting to it; I was only saying that it is strange the attraction of things that are harmful. Why would you drink something to such an extent, knowing that it will do you harm? Why would you smoke something, knowing that it will shorten your life? The pleasure of it, I suppose. But, analytically speaking, it doesn't make sense. It is illogical and counterintuitive."

"Now I see where you are going – like the button box, you mean?"

"Exactly. The button box is like a purely rational expression of that idea. It's as though Grandfather Henry Dickson, robbed of alcohol by his Methodist upbringing, translated that principle into an idiom he could understand: carpentry. It is like a mathematical sublimation of something that heavy drinkers achieve in a state of tanked-up oblivion."

"Whatever's your poison, I guess," said John.

"And it is equally curious that something so circuitous and opaque was so fascinating to us, in a way that objects with a clear and functional purpose were not. We were no exception as boys – boys like dismantling things to see how they work. But I think we would both agree that the mechanics of a radio or a model railway were nothing compared to the button box. It was unique."

Tomas mulled over his glass of wine, searching its swilled properties for the equivalent to alchemical gold.

"I don't know what you mean exactly," said Lena, who was feeling a little lost and still trying to make sense of Tomas' note.

Tomas ignored her; he continued to draw inspiration from his wine. If she looked closely, Lena could see that the furrowed attention Tomas gave to his drink and his apparent musing over this paradox occupied only half his mind. She sensed that the centre of his thoughts was some way ahead of his pensive interest in the contents of his glass and that his hanging over the rim of his wine glass was only a gesture calculated for dramatic effect.

Tomas, as if he had been waiting for this quiet observation, looked at her intently, in the same way he had looked at her only a few minutes earlier.

"There is a story about a primeval sphere, the surface of which was simple, comprised of the most basic elements: it was covered only in water. You could not say that the sphere was untroubled any more than it was troubled or calm any more than it was restless as these words could only ever apply to a more heterogeneous scenario. The sphere remained in this simplistic state until a demonic demiurgic principle of creation in the form of a bird dived into the waters of the sphere and fished out of them land, mountains, the first flora, the basis for a flourishing biosphere of life. The first creatures evolved from these basic elements of creation and cleverly duplicated the first act of creation repeatedly so that over time they formed communities, they learned to catalogue and understand the world around them, they developed cities, transportation, forms of subsistence, and later, models for sustainable economic growth; they created culture and language, a sense of history, tradition and identity; they developed property, rules about the way in which their society should grow and be governed; they tacked on wacky ideas like urban development, house-warming parties, and gardens. But at the root of this spiralling circle of absurdity was the initial conceited act of creation, the vestige of which and the principle of which flourishes and proliferates *ad infinitum.*"

"Damn birds," said Lena. "I bet it was a pigeon."

"So this story is a model," continued Tomas.

"What do you mean, a model?"

"The technical word is 'cosmogony'."

"Cosmogony," repeated Lena moronically.

"But is it a *hermetic* cosmogony?" asked John.

Lena looked obstructed. Unhindered air flowed through her open mouth and stymied her vocal chords. Her normal effusion of careless thoughts were cornered and incarcerated. It was a look that searched forlornly for a single object of charity in her hour of need: a dictionary.

"The story turns everything on its head. It is like a freakish acrobat walking on his hands. But only *like* a freakish acrobat walking on his hands. Because the story could never allow that this is, in fact, the correct way to walk. Any more than your right hand is your left or that a portrait in monochrome is a portrait in colour. That would be two easy. The story would not approve of someone for whom their right hand was their left hand but only the sense of surprise, of disorientation, frustration and anxiety this might occasion in the unsuspecting spectator. The story is like a mischievous monarch decreeing that the proletarian diet for the past five years was not cake but fish heads that only looked like cake! It is a permanent act of subterfuge."

"Why? I don't understand," said Lena.

"Well, let's say there was a family. The family lived in a house in the north of England – for the sake of argument, let's say they lived in Yorkshire. Family members lost many buttons from their shirts, dresses and trousers in the course of their life in the house. They fell off here and there. Some disappeared without the owners of the garment noticing and turned up later, behind the bachelor's chest or down the side of a wing-back armchair, or among the bed springs after of a round of particularly fierce frottage. The house was decorated in lost buttons. The brickwork was practically cemented with them. So a thoughtful and organised person – probably a grandmother – thought practically; she decided that it would be sensible to store all the miscellaneous buttons together in a box, so that there would always be a selection of buttons to replace those that went missing. And she asked her husband – who worked as a carpenter – to build a box to store the buttons. This idea was practical and logical. It might even seem like a good idea. Where there were once buttons strewn about the place willy nilly, in the age of the button box this would all change. It was an inspired creation.

'But the husband was a man with an exploratory conscience and hands chafed and callused by craft. He saw the need for a button box, for a system, a catalogue, an archive of buttons. He had spent years subordinating his skill to the requirements of similar jobs. He could rub his hands over the grain of many ideas to which he had given concrete form: parquetry, rafters, beams, trusses. In all these cases he had used his craft to build or to manifest an idea with a clear and practical application; but in this case – perhaps there was a little autumnal water on his brain? – it occurred to him that he might put his craft to a different use. Suppose the core idea were different; suppose he were to create something the purpose of which was not to facilitate access to buttons in the right sizes, shapes and colours. Suppose he were to create an object for losing buttons, for concealing them, even erasing them. Suppose he were to confound the logic of creation. Suppose he were to unravel it. In the language of the cosmogony, suppose he were to undo the work of the earth-diving bird and drown it. And that's what he did – in a crafted form, in something you could touch, in something you could observe, in something to which you could apply your intelligence."

"The grandmother probably gave him a thwack with her rolling pin!" said Lena.

Lena muscled in on a pocket of silence. She often sat through her uncle's explanations wishing for a verbatim transcript of their conversation from which she might extract a piece-by-piece analysis of his thoughts. It seemed strangely unfair that he spoke so fluently and thoughtfully about such matters. She consoled herself quietly with the belief that these speeches were all rehearsed in some way, like a performance (they often sounded like a performance). She tried to work out the exact relationship between the story of the bird and the button box and, in thrall to an otherwise comatose instinct to sleuth, she tried to relate them both to Henry's disappearance. But she was distracted by Tomas' beard. It didn't suit him. It made him look like a fat man in a thin man's body. And he had caught a grain of barley in it.

"So you have had the button box in your loft all this time, John?"

Tomas asked the question as though it was an opening gambit in a complex game the three of them were about to start playing.

"Yes."

"I never knew. You never told me you had taken it."

"I'm sorry, Tomas. I didn't think you'd care. I think I ... yes, I think I did try to contact you at the time to let you know about ... to let you know I was dealing with mother and father's belongings. It was shortly after the funeral. You said that you were ... I think you told me ... I'm sure in fact that you told me to do whatever I ... you said you had no ..."

"Yes, I know that but, even so, I would have been interested to have another look at the button box. We did, after all, think of it as a kind of magic; it kept alive the rumour of our family history. It would be interesting to see what we might find in the box."

"I had no idea you were ... I mean you have never showed much ... but of course I am sure you are ..."

"It strikes me that you were a little thoughtless."

"Well I ... I did mention ... I did offer."

"You never mentioned the button box."

"Look, if you would like to have a look at ... if you would like to keep it, you can ... on the condition that you leave the box to Lena. She would perhaps like to … as she said … it would be nice, like you say, to keep the rumour alive. So, if you … I will arrange to send it over to you. It's no great problem. It's just in the loft."

"Rotting, no doubt."

"It's just in the loft with the rest of the stuff I kept from … from the house."

Tomas stared at his brother with the same hard, inflexible expression. He jabbed his fork at the bone of lamb that was left on his plate, and then took another drink from his wine. He knocked it back like a short. Just as swiftly he leaned over his plate and attacked the remnants of his meal. John looked flustered by his brother's behaviour and Lena gazed at Tomas, mouth wide open and her mind stretched to the limits of curiosity. She was still half-distracted by the grain of barley in Tomas' beard.

"Why were you never interested in it?"

"What do you mean?"

"You only wanted … you were only interested in counting the fucking buttons! Our great-great-great grand-father had gone to painstaking time and detail and all you ever wanted was to take out all the buttons and sort them into neat little piles. What about the structure of it? What about the concept of it?"

"We are different characters."

"Yes! You're a piggy bank! And you never cared about the family! Everything clusters around you but you do absolutely nothing with it and beyond that there's nothing more to you. You squirrel away! You accumulate buttons! But you're not interested in the 'how' and 'why'. Just the fucking buttons! Why did you keep it? You don't care about it."

"I'm sorry, Tomas. As I say, you can have it."

"But why don't *you* want it?"

"I guess it means more to ... "

"*You* never cared about the family, Tomas!" said Lena sternly. "You were always somewhere else, travelling or something ..."

"The box is, of course, very complicated," continued John. "But you know ... you are aware that you have exaggerated. We all ... I have exaggerated. We liked to believe that it was more complicated and mysterious than it is."

"But that's it! That's just it, you puritanical prick! That's why it mattered! But for you it didn't matter! For you it was 'not that complicated'. For you it was a cash dispenser! Or a filing cabinet that helped to pass the time!"

"We are different, that's all," said John bluntly.

Lena had seen Tomas behave like this before. She had witnessed him – usually in public – make a scene or kick up a fuss, which caught the guarded attention of everyone in the vicinity. He would direct his scene-making powers at anyone, personal or impersonal; but several times now, she had seen him work his inverted charm on John. He appeared to enjoy prodding John where he felt most vulnerable; this included anything that involved the family. She could not understand Tomas' behaviour and because she could see no good reason for it, she thought it was unfair and mean, which made her angry. The first time he had attacked John in this way, she had been too stunned to say anything. It was only when a pattern started to emerge that she felt obliged to stick up for him, particularly since he never did it himself.

Tomas was especially mean, she thought, because he chose the family as the subject of his assault and because her father was unhappy to use the family as any kind of ammunition in his defence.

"How can you say these things?!" she said with a strained voice. "Dad was always there for the family! He looked after … he spent years looking after them! But you were never there! So, who gives a shit about the button box?! We even asked you if you could help out looking after them and you said you were busy. You weren't even in a play or anything! You weren't even teaching! You were on holiday in Mexico! And…," she said groping blindly through fury, "… and you have barley in your beard!"

IV

There was in the centre of the town a small market square. Periodically – sometimes fortnightly, sometimes monthly – a market appeared; it sold food, clothes and a raft of miscellaneous items: Turkish rugs, laughing Buddhas, Bavarian beer and sausage. The square was deserted for most of the time. There was a small car-parking area, demarcated by white lines painted over busted-up concrete. Lena would cut through the square on her way to one of many places, but most of her friends preferred to take longer routes via the main road. They didn't like the exposure of a wide open space, particularly at night.

Lena had never really understood the worries of her friends; they all seemed to assume that there was a network of petty crime operating twenty-four hour surveillance of the square. The square was beat-up and decrepit, but there was no history of horror to justify a reputation for notoriety.

In the week leading up to her evening with her father and her uncle, she met a lady in one of the narrow alleyways that fed into the square. When the lady looked up at her with dew in her eyes and said that a man had stolen her handbag, an underworld army of recidivist rapists, murderers, thieves, drug addicts and other boot-high scumbags became the object of her mind's eye. A place that only needed someone in authority to throw some spare change and a sweeping brush at it became, in a flash, a sprawling wasteland of moral detritus.

Lena did not recognise the lady; she had Nordic height and elegance, disarranged and flustered by the trauma of her experience. Her hair, an edible blonde like white chocolate, was tied back in a ponytail, which exposed an imprint of tension creased into her forehead. On first catching sight of her, Lena had expected to see cuts, bruises, blood, but, up close, she showed only a loss of colour and a thin glaze of sweat. Lena, who had noticed the woman's distress from a distance, walked up to her and asked her what the matter was. The woman looked back at her.

"Someone has stolen my handbag. I was just walking into the high-street and he jumped out. He stole my handbag. I thought he was going to ..."

Lena sat down beside the woman and offered support. Her name was Saskia Delaney. She lived outside the town in a small village called Edgerton. Her husband was a lawyer with the Crown Prosecution Service. From a distance, the stylish wrap of her clothes and model figure made her look young, but she was much older than she appeared. Something more than colour had disappeared from her face; she looked tired.

Lena suggested that they should walk to the police station and report the theft but Saskia refused. She said she would like to take a moment to clear her head. If any information she could provide were to be of any use to the police, it would need to be coherent at the very least. She was not, so close in time to the crime, coherent. Top of her list of priorities was a cigarette. Lena explained that she did not smoke but that she would be happy to buy Saskia a packet.

Lena suggested that they pull up a pew outside *The Dirty Café*, where Saskia could get her nicotine fix and find time to compose her recollection of events. Saskia accepted the offer without hesitation.

In the sitting area outside the café, Saskia smoked hungrily through one of the cigarettes from the packet Lena had bought as her coffee went cold. Once she had stubbed out the cigarette she looked at the dead filter among the small pile of ash and reached immediately for another. She talked as she smoked and raced through an account of how she had come to be in the area. She had been to the gym at the leisure centre and was about to visit the bank before she returned to her car in the market square.

"There is a school not so far from here," she said. "A teacher once caught a group – though they were more of a pack – getting their thrills. Do you know how they got their thrills?"

"How?"

"By kicking to death a rabbit with myxomatosis. For fun."

Lena was not often left searching for something to say; in most situations a thought – however vacant and whimsical – would enter her brain and she would broadcast it, usually to an audience of confused indifference. Saskia's words did not tease out the strange leaps of internal logic that words usually exercised upon Lena. It was ironic since words were usually the means through which she could happily enjoy hours of frivolous personal contact; but Saskia's words were like an injunction to share a bipartisan moment of respectful silence. They were an opportunity to reflect (with just enough time to reach a condemning judgement).

Lena reflected. She interrogated the ash tray and the mottled carpet of ash despoiling the glass base. She pictured the crease of aggression across the gang's collective face as it played football with the poor rabbit. She had once overheard a teenager in Leeds trading antisocial capital on a bus. He could not have been more than fourteen or fifteen. He had a squashed head compressed awkwardly onto industrial slabs of flesh and frontal lobes that pulsated with a beat of anger; the hormonal fluff of a moustache was budding across his upper lip. He looked like an apprentice to a hit man.

The crucial point to keep in mind when 'kicking the shit' out of someone, explained the neophyte delinquent, was to avoid too much contact with the head.

"It's not like yer wanna to get sent down for murder!" he joshed.

Lena had found it hard to imagine anyone mothering this strangely misshapen creature. He was the sort of child wrenched uncaringly into the space-time continuum asexually; a creature that might have wandered out of a landfill fully formed. But she knew that the mother-son relationship was integral to the psychology of crime and so she had envisaged the boy retiring after a day of hard-won head-kicking to a docile parent who mopped the beads of anger from his choleric forehead with a cool tea-towel.

"It's spreading, you know: crime," said Saskia. "It's taking root in this town. Once it establishes a grip ..."

She said it was to be expected the way the government was carrying on. You only had to look elsewhere to see the way crime was spreading. Crime – 'serious' crime – was no longer confined to the inner cities. Organised gangs and criminals had wised up; they had discovered new ways of operating, new infrastructures, new markets and commodities. East Yorkshire – particularly in and around Driffield – was fast becoming a problem area for drugs, mainly crack-cocaine. It was the same as the other places that had become the subject of special documentaries on television: the drug dealers offered a ten pound hit first time round and then notched up the price. This meant that a new wave of petty thieves were crawling the streets, hungry for their exorbitant high.

The theft of her handbag was significant. It signified the beginning of the end. Soon, as such robberies became more frequent and as the thieves found their confidence, there would emerge no-go areas; the town would be too worried to enter certain parts and the criminal fraternity would mark their territory clearly. The police would chase light-footed law-breakers through the streets into these criminal mouse holes, places into which the police would never be able to follow without proper arms or entering a labyrinth of bureaucratic self-justification. She had heard and read about such districts first-hand from her husband and second-hand in the newspapers, in topical books and 'informed' double-page spreads. Leeds had, for some time, been home to many similar neighbourhoods; and it was only common sense to suppose that there was some overspill. There was probably a clandestine motorway of dirty traffic running from coast to coast across the whole of northern England.

"We shall have to move," she said breathlessly. "We shall have to move to Harrogate."

Police officers, of all the professional bodies who dealt with crime, came closest to the phenomena itself; her husband had often observed a 'distant chumminess' between police officers and known felons. Criminologists, criminal psychologists and other expert students of the criminal mind had identified behavioural patterns and stitched together a threadbare fabric of cause and effect; but there were certain cases where the criminals did their utmost to confound the combined efforts of the experts.

There was a girl, it seemed. She went by various names because no-one in the public sphere knew her real name. The authorities who became involved in the investigation of her murder conjectured that she descended from Bulgaria; some of the tenant farms in the region and a number of small factories relied heavily on seasonal migrant workers from eastern Europe, many of whom came from Bulgaria. The police and the investigating authorities concluded that she had been brought into the country through these established channels.

She had never worked on a farm or in a factory. She had never showed up on the payroll of any organisation in the region. The evidence suggested that, like many other girls, a 'friendly' patron had offered to pay her fare to the country. The coroner found that she had suffered a form of pelvic inflammatory disease which led to the view that she had been coerced into prostitution. The coroner also recorded severe lacerations on her left arm, including several that looked like a prisoner's tally of days.

The police had found evidence to suggest that she had lived (and 'worked') in one of the town's old council flats in Mossholme Yard.

"It wouldn't surprise me," said Saskia stiffly.

The police interviewed local residents for details about the life of the girl but the evidence was scant. Testimonies were either naive about her existence or reticent. Several neighbours claimed they had seen a man going in and out of the flat once or twice. The descriptions they gave varied so much that they only compounded the search.

"With no public records, little in the way of forensic evidence and only a slither of anecdotal evidence, the police were left pursuing even the smallest and most unlikely leads," explained Saskia.

Saskia rubbed the palm of her hand across her forehead, smearing the thin film of make-up over the pores of her skin.

"So there was this girl …" she continued.

Her body had rotted and decayed by the time the police found her. Welts and other lesions damaged the puckered rag of white skin left on her flesh and bones. Her hair had thinned and her eyes were retreating into her sockets, leaving behind the first impressions of her hollowed skull. Areas of her torso and her thighs had started to swell. A blue tincture spread across parts of her skin and engulfed scars and contusions.

The police surmised that the murder was no arbitrary act; they took it as probable that she was the victim of someone in the coterie of organised crime for whom she had worked. They liaised closely with other constabularies around the country and pooled information from a national database of criminal profiles.

"I believe they pieced together several possible groups and a handful of individuals who they regarded as suspicious. But the most concrete lead was the most unusual."

Six months after the discovery of the girl's body a man came to the police. He worked for a recruitment agency in Leeds through whom one of the meat factories south of the town recruited foreign workers. He told them that he was acting at the request of a woman formerly employed at the factory who had since returned to eastern Europe and refused to come back. The man gave the police two items of evidence: a letter written by the woman in her native Polish and a photograph. The police had the letter translated. In it the woman alleged that she knew the perpetrator of the murder, that she had seen him with the girl many times before she was killed, and that she had enclosed his picture.

"The picture she enclosed was not a photograph but a daguerreotype, a black and white picture of a man in a rough-collar shirt with a moustache and brylcreemed hair. The police, though they could not take this allegation seriously, ran a search on the identity of the man. His name was Arthur Caulfield. He had been a police officer at the same constabulary in the early twentieth century. And it was believed that he had murdered his wife, here in this town, before disappearing from the public eye."

A morose and intense kind of possession governed Saskia's manner and bearing. A radial bead of light bore through her eyes and the sunken fatigue that surrounded them. She reached for her words through short gasps of air that lived on the edge of suffocation. Her fingertips stroked the rim of the ashtray, like the proboscis of a mosquito probing for blood. She fitted the picture of a moth-eaten puppet in its last live performance jerked about frantically by the demonic will of a concealed puppeteer.

"The collation of evidence is a slow process. Evidence is about logic. There are numerous cases in which the police can identify known criminals but are unable to match their profile to specific felonies. So justice requires a system. Evidence is recorded, given official status, and professionals – like my husband – analyse the information that the police have collated and assess whether they can bring a case before the courts. Each piece of evidence has to be scrutinised and tested for ambiguities, nuances of meaning and interpretation. But crime can take advantage of those ambiguities; it can – and often does – ride roughshod through a legal lacuna or administrative elision. And the more elliptical the crime the easier it is for the criminal to slip through the clumsy, clunking hands of the law."

"So what are you saying?" asked Lena.

"Well, suppose it's true. Suppose this Arthur Caulfield did murder the girl."

"But that's not possible ... is it? He would be too old."

"But how could the law possibly bring him to trial? As you say, it defies common sense and the law is based on principles of common sense. If it were true, if he did murder the girl, it would be a kind of perfect crime. It would make him untouchable."

Saskia leaned low over the table so that Lena could see down her cleavage. Her eyes squinted and her index finger, full of the same manic sense of purpose, made demands of the Formica. Her mind, body and their combined reactions were still riding out an adrenalin roller. There was so much information and detail amassing in her head that she could not find a vehicle for its expression. She could not keep still; she shuffled about in her seat. She turned her chair so that it was parallel to the length of the table and crossed her legs repeatedly.

"Of course, these are myths. Stories. They have come crawling out of the woodwork. I mean, they are nonsense, of course. But crime relies on myths. Crime, in order to survive, has to conceal itself in some way. That's what I mean. That's how criminals become untouchable: by surrounding themselves in mystery. They use these kind of stories; they take advantage of them. But the key thing, the thing that you have to keep in mind, is that there are real people behind the stories. And it is the role of the law to unravel these myths and identify the criminals. So, what I am saying is that there are organisations, groups – call them what you will – who are operating in this part of the world and who are exploiting this mythology. But the more these stories gain prominence the more you can be sure that crime is on the rise."

Crime was spiralling out of control in the world that Saskia described. Lena could loosely understand the causal connection Saskia was trying to relate but she could not *picture* the connection; she could not see the node that joined to civil disobedience and the upward arching graph of unlawful behaviour. But, she supposed, that was the point.

In Saskia's view, a whole generation of angry frontal lobes loomed over the horizon. Hormonal adolescents, thickset and misshapen, contorted and bent by the ripening hatred, hostility and appetite for anarchy that spurred them on, would dominate the streets. The government and public organisations, like schools, social services and church-run charities, would be forced to stem the oncoming tide. She envisaged a programme of reform. Long queues of head-kickers and handbag-stealers would form outside government-funded inoculation clinics run by redoubtable nurses with fat arms and heaving bosoms. The boys would be strapped forcefully into a chair and the nurses would puncture their inflated foreheads with a three-inch needle, after a short but determined run at the patient. In the age of bilious boy the nurse with the needle would be at the vanguard of law and order.

This was the great crisis of the current generation. Where the country had once grown potatoes and baked homemade carrot cake to fend off the jackbooted Wehrmacht, people of conscience needed to come together once more to excise the menace from within. There might be a league of young women who could offer the latter-day equivalent to bandages and clean sheets to the troubled youth of the present. In the post-apocalyptic future, there might be hospitals of lobotomised patients dribbling into bibs and grinning insanely in the aftermath of their suppressed violence. Men, Lena had concluded after some years of experience, always needed some form of personal care.

Lena had never held a conversation with a lobotomy patient. She imagined that there would not be much room for manoeuvre and the conversation would be lopsided, confined to monosyllabic words like 'sponge', 'fork', 'mash' and 'chew'. She calculated the extent to which she could endure wet afternoons spent playing condescending games of four-letter scrabble with patients missing chunks of their brain. It would test her resolve.

And then there would be the clinical fallout; there would have to be a central science laboratory somewhere in the bucolic heart of Hampshire stacked high with bits of brain pickled in glass jars, upon which febrile scientists would conduct experiments to track down the biological cause of the rabid-like illness.

"Do you know what they say about the policeman?" asked Saskia.

"No."

"That you know him through his actions, through nervous gestures of the body, grinding teeth, the sounds he makes indirectly rather than direct speech."

"Uh huh," said Lena thoughtlessly.

V

Saskia cleared her throat and drew another cigarette from her packet. She looked more composed now. Her thoughts appeared to have settled and she relaxed into her chair.

"I have heard bits of information that would make your toes curl," said Saskia. "Of course they are only rumours and really I should not discuss them with you. Not that it's wrong. I mean, not that it's improper. These stories ... well who knows where they come from. That's why I suppose it's not strictly right to tell you .... This girl I told you about. The Bulgarian girl ..."

"Yes."

"I heard she was a very beautiful girl. She had a fine figure; eye-catching, shall we say. And she caught the eye of almost every 'gentleman' that fetched eyes on her. So, as you can imagine, she was never out of work, so to speak. I think the person who told me the story said she worked every day. Her guardians expected her to earn so much each day. It wouldn't surprise me."

Saskia paused. She seemed to be working out how to narrate the sequence of events and questioning whether or not she had everything in the right order. She gave a peculiar sigh. It sounded like a hushed elephant call.

"The girl had regular clients. I've heard this is par for the course; men are nothing if not habitual creatures. Some of them even brought her flowers and other gifts. They would even talk about their lives at home, about their wives and children. Some of them would take her out to dinner, to restaurants or to the theatre. One man paid for her to travel down with him to Covent Garden.

'There was a regular client from the town who became very interested in the girl. The person who told me the story didn't say much about this person; she suggested that he was some kind of local trafficker in narcotics with strong ties to the organisation that had brought the girl over. This person visited her regularly and he liked asking her about her family and her home in Bulgaria. He asked her what she thought of her new life. She said it was fine. He did not believe her and so he asked her again what she thought of her new life. She told him again that it was fine. He asked her if she missed her family. She said she missed them a bit.

'An exchange began to take place between the girl and the criminal. He wanted to know more about her; he wanted to know more about her life in Bulgaria and more about how she reacted to her life in England. He said that, if she wanted, he would stop visiting her and stop asking her questions. She said that she didn't want it.

'"Why is that?" the man once asked her. "Why do you want to see me? Because I want to know the truth? Because you want to be free?"

'The girl said she was content with her position.

'After several months the man would no longer use her for sex. He only wanted to talk; so he visited her on the pretext of their original arrangement and instead they stayed locked in a room, where the man asked her questions and they ate pastries and yoghurt together. One of their favourite places to meet was in bookshops. They would arrange to meet in the cookery section or the poetry section. Imagine that! There they were looking up exotic recipes and flicking through verses from renaissance poets!

'He told her that he wanted her to feel as if she could trust him, but that he recognised she probably never would. She loosened up slightly; she asked him if he could sing a traditional song from her part of Bulgaria to him.

'She received a message the following day from the criminal, asking her to meet him at an anonymous location in the town. She was told that she should meet him at ten in the evening. The criminal sent her a car and an escort to guide her to the meeting room. The room was a large high-ceilinged room. There was no sign of the criminal when she walked in. The room was empty except for a strange-looking piece of machinery at the far end of the room. I am not clear myself what this machinery looked like. There was some sort of metal frame. Some kind of instrument was attached to the top of the frame. The girl walked over to the machinery to examine it. Up close, she could see that the instrument looked like several large sets of fangs sticking out from a crescent-shaped base. On either side of the instrument were small holes, each about six centimetres in diameter. When she looked closely at the fangs she saw that they were needles filled with some kind of liquid. She reached out to touch one of the needles, when a shape strayed across the corner of her eye. The criminal was leaning against the wall.

'"What is it?" she asked the criminal, referring to the machine.

'"I could show you if you like."

'"Why? What is it?" she asked.

'"I brought you here so that I could give you a choice. For all this time you have been imprisoned in this town; you have been forced into slavery; you have been forced to sell your body against your will; you have suffered shame and humiliation; you have been beaten, abused, robbed and cheated; you have incurred great debts and fallen victim to men who would as soon murder you as they would take advantage of you. For a time every single part of you wanted to escape. Now, I have come to think that this miserable life of yours has crushed almost every spark of hope out of you. But it is at this time, that I want to offer you a choice. The choice is simple: either you can remain in your current predicament as a prostitute and slave, or I can show you how this machine works."

'"Why? What does it do?" she asked.

'"I will say nothing. The choice is yours," he replied.

'"It looks nasty," she said, looking at the machine.

'The criminal walked up to her and undid a latch that hooked the instrument to the top of the metal frame.

'"It is," he said.

"'But good?" she asked.
"'Perhaps."
'The girl looked over the machine once more. The instrument and its needles were attached to three mechanical arms secured at the top four corners of the metal frame. These arms could extend and retract so that the criminal could either lower or raise the instrument. He had pulled the instrument closer to them so that she could get a closer look at the needles. When it moved it followed the downward trajectory of an arc, so that it moved out towards the edge of the metal frame and then swiftly back towards the centre.

"'What's in the needles?" she asked.

"'I will not tell. You must make your choice. I will give you one more minute to decide."

"'There's no need; I have already decided," she said hurriedly. "I will see how your machine works."

'The criminal smiled.

"'That's what I thought," he said.

'And then he grabbed hold of the girl forcefully by the arms and thrust her inside the metal frame of the machine.

"'What are you doing?" she asked in alarm.

'The man, still holding her firmly by the arms, looked hard at her.

"'You have decided. And that's final. There is no going back now. I think it would be best for you if you accept it. It is worse for some people. Some people don't accept it. Some people like to scream. Do you understand me?"

'The girl looked back at him and then she nodded her head.

'"Yes."

'The criminal raised her arms and fitted her hands into the two small holes at the top of the metal frame. With each hole he used a screw to narrow the diameter and prevent her from retrieving her hand. He used two leather straps at the base of the frame to secure her legs. The criminal checked that she was properly fastened into the contraption and then he turned his attention to the instrument. He pulled the instrument down slightly. There was a click as the instrument appeared to lock into position. The criminal walked away from the machine and from his coat pocket he pulled a remote control. He looked at the girl once more. Her attention shifted away from the needles. She looked at the man, waiting for his next move.

'"Are you ready?" he said.

'"Yes," she replied.

'The man pushed a button on his remote control and the metal frame began to vibrate. The mechanical arms came to life; they pushed the instrument downwards; there were a further two clicks and then it moved smoothly, three quarters of the way through the crescent-shaped trajectory, like a crouched animal waiting to pounce. The girl followed the movement of the instrument obsessively. There was a sound of bolts coming undone. The whole machine went silent when this sound had stopped. The frame stopped vibrating. Everything stood still for a moment. The instrument rushed through the air without making a sound so that the girl barely had time to register what was happening. First it moved out towards the edge of the frame and then back into the centre. There, the five needles stabbed her violently in her lower abdomen. The sudden impact of the needles winded her, and she exhaled a single gasp of air.

'The girl and the instrument stayed locked together for some time. She is supposed to have smiled for the first minute or two until her whole body started to shake. She started to make choking noises. She retched up a combination of blood and vomit. She stayed like this, just shaking and vomiting up blood and sick for a further two minutes. The frame began to vibrate and the mechanical arms pulled the instrument and its needles out of her body. It moved slowly up through the same arc to the top of the frame. The girl hung dead, as limp as grass."

Lena looked at Saskia suspiciously who took a long drag from a cigarette; Lena was wary of the story and wary of Saskia's motives for telling it. A waitress wiped down the table opposite.

"I'm sorry if I have upset you," said Saskia. "I only wanted to let you know something of the danger. I've got to tell you, though, that I don't believe the account is true. Not for a minute. It's folklore. Pure folklore. But the person – my friend – who told it to me, said something very important. She said that is based in fact. As I have already said, people may have distorted it over time and added in gory details, but the account of events comes from somewhere; it has a history and an origin. It reflects something real.

It reflects something that is going on in this region, in this town. And we have every reason to be scared."

VI

Tomas, though he had arrived late, left early. He made an excuse – something to do with meeting an ex-pupil early the following morning – and left the room like an unsettled housefly. Lena and her father were left to clear up. Though they were now only at the far end of winter, the room had steamed up and all that was left of their recent hot air now dripped down the window in the form of condensation.

Lena and John carried the empty plates from the table through to the kitchen sombrely and without speaking. Both had, in their own way, turned quiet after the argument with Tomas. John filled the washing bowl with hot water and washing-up liquid, preparing to set to work on the many dirty pots and pans that Lena had used in preparation for their meal. Lena always liked to make full use of her cooking utensils. She saw that there was no room for efficiency; a kitchen was a like an orchestra and there was no reason to compose a piece for orchestra which made no use of the brass section or the wind instruments.

While her father washed up, Lena opened a window in the living room, and then returned to the kitchen where she boiled the kettle. Hardly a word had passed between them since Tomas had left, and they remained in silence until all the washing up and drying up had been completed. They returned to the living room, each with a cup of tea.

It was, by now, half eleven. Lena asked her father if he was tired; but John said that he wasn't at all tired. He felt quite wide awake, as though he might make it through to the morning with enough energy in store for the day ahead.

"I don't know ... if I'm honest, I don't know of a way to handle my brother," he said. "But that was a wonderful meal, all the same."

"I wonder why he invited himself along?" asked Lena.

John was not the sort of person to complain; when wounded, he retreated inside his shell. It was the flip side of his otherwise bumbling personality. She rarely saw him like this; it only happened when he was really troubled by something; and usually it was in relation to something about which he could do very little. After Lena's mother had died when Lena was in her early teens, Lena would sometimes find her father in a similar mood. She would creep out of bed to find him sitting on the sofa, doing nothing other than raking through his thoughts. It seemed to Lena that her father, in most situations, took a charitable attitude in the hope that it might elicit a positive response; but there were times when the situation was determined to confound his efforts. Tomas was increasingly that situation. And the unknown reason for it was the cause of John's reticent sofa-sitting.

A conversation between Lena and John opened up gradually and they talked through till twelve, at which time John and Lucinda returned from the pub; they heard the door shut and voices laughing in the hallway. The couple were only through their own door five minutes before the first shout ricocheted off the walls and sent a hollow shiver through the plumbing.

"Do they always do this?" asked John.

"They do it a lot."

"How do you put up with it? I would have to ask them to show some respect."

"No, I don't mind. I find it quite relaxing. In fact, if I heard nothing at all, I think I would be more worried. Do you hear that? You can hear it … it's just ahead of the shouting; that noise."

"It's coming from above, isn't it?"

"Yes, I think so. I can't work out what it is. It starts whenever Mark and Lucinda have an argument. Always. I think it must be someone upstairs. I think they have figured out a way of shutting out the arguing. I've got no idea what it is. Or what it could be. It's weird. Don't worry; it won't last. As soon as Mark and Lucinda finish, the noise will stop. It always does."

The whistler

I

Lena often saw the early morning; she shared the purchase of food for the restaurant with the sous chef. She had to be up early to get the best buys and find the sellers while they still had something of value to offer. *Freshness* was the keyword. The food had to be fresh and to acquire fresh food meant early selection. For three days in the week she pushed back the covers at five thirty or six in the morning and made one of several journeys, either in the town or beyond. On almost every other day, she slept long and late, like a slow infusion into a murky roux.

Lena could not cope without sleep; on the few days that she received less than her bare minimum – eight hours – she stopped functioning. If she did not get the amount of sleep she needed at night, her body clawed it back in the day. She had dozed off in public toilets, on buses, trains and in cafes. Twice she had woken up in *The Dirty Café* after an unplanned late night out, and once she had fallen asleep at work, in the changing room next to the walk-in refrigerator; she woke up to the cry of "Burning!"

Climbing out of bed was always an effort, no matter what the day or what time she had to get up. The bed – any bed – was a comfort. When she woke up each morning, her body felt heavy and the duvet in which she was wrapped added to the weight. The bed and the duvet had adapted to the shape of her body; they had almost started to merge. She imagined that the longer she stayed in bed the harder it would be to break away. If she stayed there long enough, her body and her bed would become inseparable and she would mark the first in a new evolutionary species: the bed lady. She would be a freak, considered too weird to place before the eyes of distinguished ladies and gentlemen, but a valuable commodity in the currency of contraband.

For anyone who had never met her before, sleeping seemed to be Lena's default activity; all other activities required some effort. Apart from falling asleep regularly in the pub after her evening shifts, she had made a habit of falling asleep in other people's apartments and houses. She had fallen asleep in Mark and Lucinda's flat so many times that Mark and Lucinda started to see their flat as Lena's second home. She had fallen asleep in public parks on sunny afternoons; she had fallen asleep in libraries and art galleries; she once fell asleep on a school visit to a Buddhist monastery while she was supposed to be meditating. Lena said she was being 'mindful of her bed'.

Lena even needed propping up as she walked home at night or as her friends clustered in the small geometric serving area of *The Big Noodle*. Her friends would spoon feed her chow mein or spring rolls as she flopped in one of the fixed-base stools that looked out onto the street, the air vaguely redolent of malt and vomit.

She became puerile and eyesore if she could not get any sleep. She was never irritable or shouted at anyone. Instead she settled on silence and introspection. She hurried through preparation head down and with a heavy frown darkening her brow. She would confuse mushrooms with shallots, rillettes with houmous, burn the fingers of the potwash as she dropped hob-hot frying pans into the industrial-sized basin and forget where to store the white wine. She would wipe sweat from her world-weary face as she navigated the traffic of the cramped kitchen.

People often commented on Lena's permanent exhaustion but whenever someone quizzed her about it, the reason she always gave was her job. Her job was physically exhausting. Increased fitness and a lower consumption of alcohol would make little difference, she insisted. The job was tiring. The way Lena figured it, she had earned the right to be lazy in her spare time. She was not lazy by nature. She had come to 'appreciate' the comfort of sleep whenever it was available.

Her long and late mornings in bed never ended when she woke up; she would rise, make her way to the kitchen, where she would fix a cup of coffee, some toast and maybe some cereal, and then she would return to bed, where she leafed through magazine articles and took up the thread of their ideas and suggestions, their visions and theories, in her own way.

She enjoyed reading the health and fashion supplements in the weekend papers; she glanced over the elegant curve of shapely bottoms in the context of recommended diets, foods to avoid and those considered 'safe'. The photographs of archetypal models splashed across the pages before her conjured up a world to which she often thought she would like to belong. The girls bounced, flounced and sofa-surfed the world like a bundle of fluff anointed on a million dollar cushion. They lived in palatial apartments and attended cocktail parties at which people fell into swimming pools and G-strings were lost somewhere behind the bird of paradise.

Lena would sometimes picture herself at a photo shoot in the Bahamas or the Mediterranean wearing a string bikini with her legs wrapped around a palm tree and a film of water dripping over her body.

These images appealed to something deep and instinctive within her. On one of the several occasions she had visited the Netherlands she had witnessed an adult street fair, which included a women-only topless bouncy castle. Lena felt consequentially at home with her melons jumping and jounced as, somewhere in the distance, a loud PA system hammered out the lyric 'Shake that trouser snake!"

This was a side to her personality that others — with her father and friends at the vanguard — felt she needed to hold in check.

"Otherwise," said Lucinda, "you will end up with a banana and a crotchless body stocking in Budapest."

Lena heeded the warning. For now at least, she would stick to cooking.

These days she was not sure, in any case, if her body would get through the screening process. She was confident that she had once had the figure. Many boys had told her so. She had turned many heads and diffused a lot of headstrong concentration. She had a curious soft-eyed look and a magnetic cleavage. She never tried to hook the opposite sex; in nightclubs or bars men would approach out of nowhere and at some point whisper in her ear, "You know, you are very beautiful." Lena said that men liked her 'soft edges'.

These edges, she was aware, had become both a little softer and flabbier in recent years and a little more prominent.

The time could race by lying in bed. Used cups of tea and empty cereal bowls accumulated in her bedroom, and often stayed there for weeks at a time. She could easily make it through till midday still propped up in bed. These mornings provided a necessary space in her routine in which she could fill in the blanks. The working week moved by at such a rate that she was not always able to keep abreast of all developments; and if something important had happened there would always be something she had missed, and which she would need to take up in more detail at a later date. She tabled her mornings in bed as her opportunity to do so. If there were ever something she had missed over a point of controversy, a regional development, or if Mark had ever mentioned the words 'property' and 'alienation' in close proximity to each other, she felt she needed the time and space to give the matter her full attention. She liked to work at her own pace and in a thorough way.

The argument between her father and her uncle over the button box was a matter she had hoped to think about in more detail during one of her long, untroubled mornings. But practice and intention were often disregarding rivals. The mornings provided so many distractions that she did not always possess the discipline and focus to pick up every loose thread. She liked to imagine that her mornings were an empty space in which she could choose her own timetable of events. But the reality was a little different; as soon as she opened one of her magazines or looked at the newspaper, something new struck her. She would then have to spend time processing this new chunk of data, which left less time for the growing backlog of subjects demanding her full attention. Even if she resisted papers and magazines, she would always find something in her room or about her own person, which would tease her concentration out of focus. She could stare at the small collection of nail varnish bottles collected on the top of her chest of drawers and recall the time she had painted the toenails of an ex-boyfriend blue as he slept. She could look at her legs and remember the time she had won a grab-the-surfboard-with-your-thighs contest while on holiday in Newquay.

II

"If I am right," said Tomas, "Henry was fond of telling the same story in different ways."

Lena was seated in an armchair in Tomas' front room. His apartment was sweet where Lena's was sour. The front room was a minimalist outline of a front room constructed from simple shapes. There was no clutter or mess; there were no stacks of old magazines, or clothes left lying on the floor. Everything in the apartment had a purpose. Tomas would refuse to include anything in the apartment which did not either fall into one of the existing categories of purpose or provide a new and needed purpose. Beyond the functional items – the furniture, a neat desk, the television – there were large areas of space. Lena found this disorienting. It was like she had found eternal life but could think of nothing to do in the time available.

"There was one story Henry told about a nineteenth century code used by merchant ships in the Far East. There was another story he told about a man in the town who murdered his wife and dispatched the body in the river. The first of these stories is untrue. The second, though it has undergone revisions and transformations in the course of its telling, is based in fact. But both stories are about the same set of events."

"Okay," said Lena.

"The first story runs something like this: the British merchant navy in the nineteenth century, in order to facilitate communication between vessels and to vest the competition for imperial expansion, devised a code which could be used to capture navigational trajectory, weather conditions, the transport of cargo and other practical information. The British government contracted a pastor known as a pioneer in the field of cryptology to develop the code. The requirement was twofold: for the seamen it had to be simple, meaningful and usable but impenetrable to anyone else. The pastor hit upon the idea of a map of Great Britain. He decided that he could use the relationship between different places on the map, both real and fictitious, as variables equivalent to the various scenarios that might arise at sea. A ship travelling, for example, from Manchester to London might denote a large vessel with a valuable consignment destined for a major port like Shanghai. The code could also communicate the navigational coordinates of their ships, their status and origin.

'Throughout the year 1891, a number of ships were attacked and sunk in roughly the same stretch of water; all of these ships used the code devised by the pastor to record the approach of a single unidentified craft from a north easterly direction before they sank. The code they all used to denote this craft was the name of a fictitious place in Scotland: *Bas Aberroy*."

"Yes," said Lena, as though a single light in a row of fairy lights had come on in her brain. "Yes, he mentioned that."

Tomas had leaned forward and with his finger he was drawing the outline of circles on the coffee table that separated them. The shapes he created seemed to relate to his explanation; it appeared that the way he drew the shape helped him to make sense of the facts. The circles he drew overlapped each other. Lena tried to understand; perhaps he envisaged that each circle contained certain information and the points of overlap were the links between each piece of information. But if that were the case, she could not see why he would not draw the information as a straight line of linked boxes.

"The second story is a little different: in 1918, the wife of a policeman born in the town in 1891 was murdered and found dead four days afterwards in the river. It is widely believed that the policeman committed the murder; he is supposed to have stabbed her five times in her womb after he learned that she was pregnant by another man. He disappeared at the same time that his wife was murdered and he was never seen again, but he was never the only suspect. There were two official theories: one, the policeman and his wife were murdered by an unknown killer and the body of the policeman was never recovered; two, the policeman murdered his wife and somehow he escaped. Either way, the case was never solved.

'Subsequent to this murder there have, throughout the latter part of the twentieth century, been several other disappearances in the town. In each case the body of the person that disappeared was discovered in the river with abdominal stab wounds."

Tomas had continued to trace out imaginary shapes on the coffee table; Lena, who was busily following the details of the two stories, had lost track of the geometric structures he was mapping out with his index finger. Her interest in the two activities was already placing excessive pressure on the overworked pistons of her brain. Now that he had come to the end of the second story, Tomas lifted his finger from the table like the needle of a record player escaping from the final groove, and leaned back into his armchair.

"And this is the true story?" Lena asked.

"Yes; these events, as it were, actually happened. The story about the ships, the code and the South China sea — that's just made up!"

"Just a minute," said Lena, "a policeman in the early twentieth century murdered his wife, yes?"

"That's correct."

"And these other bodies; they were all found in the river as well? Like the policeman's wife?"

"Yes, all with abdominal stab wounds."

"So are you saying ... who murdered them? ... What are you saying?"

"We will come to that. But, for the moment, I was just making the point that I think these two stories are essentially the same story told in a different way."

"But I don't understand; they are different."

"They are nominally different but substantially the same."

"What does that mean?"

Lena tried to retrace the details of each story in a comparative fashion. She struggled to juggle all the information without dropping everything, calling it quits and checking in for a sex and sangria beach holiday to recover from the stress. Details from the stories Henry had told her added fresh fruit and whipped cream to the trifle in her mind. Bearded Scotch midgets and diabolical river scientists courted her attention, marching her forlornly in the direction of a non-existent place called *Bas Aberroy*.

"It is my view that if you follow the details of each story closely you will notice that the details of the first story have been constructed to represent the details of the second, using an alternative idiom. In short, the first story symbolises the second."

"Okay …" said Lena.

"But why?"

"Why what?"

"What purpose does it serve to compose the story in these two different ways?"

"What do you mean?"

"If you have a set of events or facts that you want to communicate, what is the need for such a cryptic form of communication?"

"I don't know."

Tomas, leaning forward, his body arched like a predatory animal, dusted the surface of the coffee table once again with his finger; he addressed the table lightly, like a mathematician reviewing an extemporary effusion of calculations for small but vital flaws in the analytic whole.

"It is possible that Henry was trying to make something difficult to understand clearer."

"He wasn't very clear thinking then!" snorted Lena.

"I agree; which is why I don't think that was his purpose. But for the purposes of elucidation, suppose you have a complex idea or a complicated scenario which you have need to communicate to a wider audience who may, for one reason or another, not measure up to the complexity of the task; it is possible to communicate that idea by drawing an implicit comparison with imagery widely appreciated and understood or through a more familiar idiom. Computer scientists, for example, in order to make accessible unique data formatting in a directory structure, invoked the imagery of 'files' and 'folders'. They used the explanatory power of a simple idea to explain, albeit imperfectly, a complex idea in a way that would make it meaningful and practical to the user. So, in this instance, the symbolism resolves to a determinate meaning.

'But, in the case of Henry's stories, there is no determinate meaning. Or, at least, they do not resolve to anything that 'makes sense' in the ordinary use of the term. The significant trope in the first story is the code constructed by the pastor. In the first story, the code is used to represent the ships; it is my view that the ships are used to represent the bodies found in the river in the second story. So, in order of representation, the code represents the ships and ships represent the bodies. This means that the elusive ship signified by the term *Bas Aberroy* symbolises the murderer responsible for the victims dragged from the riverbed. Altogether the stories appear to be a rather cryptic way of indicating the repeated re-enactment of the same murder throughout the history of the town. I ask you: does *that* make sense?

"Henry's Russian doll of symbols does not make something difficult to understand easier to understand but illustrates the opposite: that these events, in some sense, cannot be understood. That he uses a code within a code is only a technical or a rhetorical conceit. There is no direct object to which the symbols refer in any determinate sense. So, in the true meaning of the stories, there are, by implication, *only* symbols."

"Okay ..." said Lena.

"There is a view," said Tomas, "that the imagination is a state of decay. Clear and distinct sensory impressions are stored away inside us in a sort of repository for data gathered from the external world; and the imagination is like a duplicitous thief of the mind that plunders this store indiscriminately and with no regard for the truth. Knowledge is, therefore, a recurrent attempt to re-discover our first impressions and operates under a puritanical ban on the imagination."

Lena had never thought about her imagination. She had once taken part in a scientific experiment at school, in which each participant had to breathe into a glass shaker and, over several days, observe the growth of their bacteria. Unlike her peers, whose experiments all developed into textbook examples, her breath developed into an unusual array of colours and thick, bushy mould. It was at this point that Lena formed the suspicion that she was biologically unusual. If an expert were to unravel the psychological helix of her imagination, she felt sure it would reveal something similarly deformed: a strange, over-nourished parasite sucking up common sense like a milkshake.

"But thieving is an infringement of possession; and perhaps the imagination is just asking how this contract of ownership was drawn up?"

Tomas' eyes were fixed on the small area he had demarcated on the coffee table and the imaginary shapes he had created. He moved the palm of his hand over the area, and then, carefully so as not to intrude upon the shapes he had already created, he drew a rectangular perimeter around the space where he had drawn the circles.

"How do you know him?" she asked eventually.

III

On some mornings it would be easier to think about ham or sweet potato. On other mornings she was too zonked or hung over to complete more than half a thought without pillowing her head from the strain. At other times, she thought about a man – or 'boy' as she preferred – who she had met one night out with her friends in Leeds. He worked in Leeds at a designer tailors. They had met in a plush bar as they ordered some drinks. Lena had looked at him curiously and then she said:

"You have nice hair!"

His hair was long, brown and curled, like decorative shavings of chocolate.

They had a long conversation about shampoo and conditioner which led into another long conversation about clothes and the best ways to rip off city types. He was a year her junior (twenty eight). He made occasional jokes which she laughed at tendentiously, but she was mainly attracted by the breadth and depth of his knowledge and interest in sartorial dress. He talked about 'room in the shoulders' and 'trouser shape'. This, she thought, showed unusual sensitivity and by the end of the evening they were snogging, like two surfaces stuck on each other in a vacuum. His name was Richard Terrier, known as 'The Terrier' to his friends. They exchanged numbers.

She thought he had a nice smile; his body was 'firm'. He had a confident erupting laugh. His eyes twinkled with mischief.

The Terrier became the subject of incomplete plots and plans; Lena often passed the time making plans for the future or simply musing over the many and various ways it might unfold. The initial stages of her relationships with men were the most interesting and exciting. Each characteristic, each physical feature was pregnant with potential. Lena liked to devise hypothetical scenarios to test how her boys might measure up, how they might endure certain challenges. Liver, she noticed, divided people greatly; many men – and women – she had met did not like liver. She had always thought that people perceived liver as a bit too close to a vital organ. Eating a leg or a breast or a piece of rump steak was safe, but the liver, she imagined, caused people to wince inwardly. The liver was only an anatomic stroll away from a heart or a lung or the bladder. But this was a fallacy; it showed a kind of weakness. Those men who liked liver were adventurous by nature; they were the sort of men who went deep-sea diving with sharks and could order shots of mescal in South American makeshift bars without feeling any kind of pretence.

Lena was not sure the Terrier ate liver but he showed potential in all sorts of areas. She had spent some time examining him closely; he had a boyish, beaming face. His mind was lively and hopped from one subject to another with a sense of unbalance and improvisation that always teetered on the edge of incoherence. Even his uneven teeth had a strange kind of appeal.

The noise continued to compete for her attention when she was not prospecting for romantic potential. It always found a way, slinking around the rusted armature of the building, to interrupt her. Wherever she was and whatever she was doing in her flat, it caught her attention when it started. She would stop to acknowledge the sound. She would lift her hand from the chopping board. She would raise her head from its focus on the television set. She would retrieve her head from the folds as she towelled her face dry. If and when it occurred, the sound would become a leitmotif in her brain, recurring between the trivial traffic to which she subjected her attention. It left an imprint on matters that she would otherwise address unsullied and influenced the nature and direction of her thoughts.

The sound crept towards her from around corners, through the clover-shaped holes in the grating, out of the cupboard in which a large house spider had colonised the water tap; it shook the weathered frame of the building through the drainpipes and entered the sound-space of her room obtrusively, divested of origin.

The sound was elusive in many different ways; Lena, in a series of incidental observations, had noticed that it suggested strange behaviours. It may have been coincidence or the play of her mind, but she had observed patterns emerging. She could begin to see an oblique order of causal connections. Events happened in concurrence with the sound; not just other noises in the building, including the arguments on the floor below, the pacing about of footsteps and the clangorous jolt of water pipes, but small, seemingly insignificant, events, tied in with the industrial thud from several floors above.

She had watched a spider spin its web in the bathroom as she leaned back in the bath. The couple downstairs were shouting, the meter-like sound above sung out stridently and the industrial life of the apartment block hummed constantly. The spider continued to weave the web until the shouts from below fell away, the noise above stopped abruptly and the building fell silent suddenly, cut off from all services. The spider waited, suspended on the edge of its web as though waiting further instruction. The building remained silent and the spider crawled across the latticework into a scar in the coving.

On a separate occasion, Lena, tense from all the noise around her and ground down and grumpy after an arduous lunchtime shift, sat by her window, her head leaning plaintively against the glass as she breathed heavy condensation. There were patches on the glass that would not steam over, and the shape of which altered with each breath. She began leaning away from the window to look at these patches in focus and she saw that they were letters. There was a clear 's', followed by an unmistakable 'o' and a 'u' and then an 'n'. The sound stopped; the argument below lost its venom and retreated into separate rooms; the building switched off. She examined the windowpane wearily and breathed on the glass. This time her breath made a steamy patch with no letter.

IV

Tomas would not reveal from where exactly Henry hailed; he allowed only a noncommittal nod towards the midlands. The place, he seemed to think, was immaterial as were so many other incidental facts about the person he claimed to know only tenuously. Tomas prefaced every subject on which he could expatiate with a denial of expertise.

Henry, at the age of twenty one and unlike many of his contemporaries, did not have any debts. He had survived three years of higher education without incurring an overdraft or facing the repayment of a loan. Six years later, he had stored away a substantial sum of money in a high-interest savings account, which saw his savings grow at a respectable rate. He had saved so much of his income after nine years of work that the balance of his current account kept on growing. Shortly after he had moved to the town, he went into the local branch of his bank in order to register his change of address and close some existing standing orders and direct debits. The customer services representative who assisted him took one look at the details of his current account towards the end of their interview.

"Do you always keep that amount of money in your current account?" she asked.

"Yeah .. no, I really must do something with it."

Henry never looked at his bank statements; he stored them away unopened in plastic bags.

He used the same 'system' for filing details of his car and home insurance policies, all the paperwork that related to the payment of his household services and council tax. He had set up direct debit payments when he had first moved in, but, beyond that, he gave it no more thought.

His attitude to his work was similar; all accounts from his colleagues suggested that he was a very conscientious worker. He showed up each day on time and followed the treadmill of hours stoically. No-one the police interviewed indicated that he was an outstanding worker or that he showed a flair and a passion for his work. He was known as reliable, productive and an efficient administrator, if a little quiet. He had not, on the other hand, made friends with anyone through his work at any of the offices at which he had worked in the last six years.

"His home was the most revealing," said Tomas.

Henry's bungalow was a mess; like all his other activities, he had made a token gesture towards a style or some kind of order. The furniture, the pictures on the wall, the lamps suggested an afternoon shopping from a catalogue; around the objects there had grown up nothing idiosyncratic, nothing to suggest the occasional sparkle, however repressed and lost to public expression, of his inner thoughts and instincts. No suggestions of even the most conventional taste or aesthetic judgement could be found. Converging on the objects in each room was a groundswell of disorder. Unopened envelopes, unread newspapers (sometimes unmoved from the carrier bag in which he had first brought them home and dating back several months), books and compact disks removed from their case, were strewn about the place. A black mould had spread in patches across his bath; the toilet, which had not been bleached possibly for as long as he had inhabited the building, stank; and limescale had formed on all the taps and the shower-head in the bathroom. He had not changed his bed linen for some time and the room smelled musty and sweaty with a hint of urine.

"Henry was not a big reader but one of the few books he owned was Wittgenstein's *Philosophical Investigations* translated into English by Elizabeth Anscombe. Some weeks before Henry had moved to the town, he had a brief conversation with a trainee lawyer on a bus – or, at least, this is what he told me. He made what seemed to me to be a rare confession. Henry told the lawyer that he had once thought about a career in the law, but that he could never understand the way lawyers battled over the smallest details of wording, as though this process winnowed out the ambiguity and established the true meaning. The trainee lawyer pointed out that the purpose was only to establish a contractual meaning; all the same, he asked if Henry had been reading Wittgenstein. Henry had never heard of Wittgenstein, but he went home and ordered a copy of the *Philosophical Investigations* online. The book arrived two weeks later by which time he had moved to the town. It would have taken one email or one phone call to have the book sent on, but he never contacted the bookseller or his former letting agent to arrange re-delivery. So Henry owns an unread copy of the *Philosophical Investigations* in another part of the country.

'You might think that this is a trivial story; but the way he treated his possessions reflects the way he treated himself. Both were left behind, discarded and largely uncared-for. If this seems like an insignificant example, I also know he allowed a month's rent to go out of his current account after he had moved out of the property; and he never claimed it back! But the story about the book is revealing. When he told me that he had never arranged to have the book moved, it was as though his entire body wilted. All the life went out of him. He became pensive, quiet and sad."

"Yes ... yes," said Lena, recognising this description from her own experience, "he was like that with me. But not all the time. He jumped. He could be, like, ... I don't know. He would switch. He was very lively at first ... well, not at first – when I first saw him he looked like that ... like you described. Then he changed. But ... I don't know ... I remember thinking that beneath it all there was just sadness and that the other things he said – all the lies he told me – were paper thin. It was the sadness that bothered me; and I warmed to that."

"You felt sorry for him?"

"I suppose."

Tomas pulled on his lip thoughtfully for a moment.

"You wanted to know how I know him – I met him ten or fifteen years ago when he was a teenager. He came to a theatre studies course I taught in the evenings. He came to the classes for a year, maybe two. He was always very keen to please, I remember and *talked* very enthusiastically about all the things he planned to do at the classes. I think his talk was really intended to please me. The classes I think he saw as a test at which he wanted to score highly, but not for himself. He just wanted to pass. It is my impression that this is how he sees most things: his job, his 'friendships', even his bank balance – they are all a kind of act of outward demonstration, an audit trail to a good public conscience. They are acts of necessity. They are calculations intended to please but they are nominal. Beyond those calculations there is nothing. They are, as you have found out, an act, a lie, an insubstantial piece of theatre. He has no personal life, no friendship – to the best of my knowledge I don't think he has ever been in love or had any intimate involvement with anyone. His personal life is like his bathtub: unkempt and overlooked."

Tomas looked at Lena for a moment; an idea appeared to have settled in his mind and he sized up the expression on Lena's face, plotting his next move.

"It is hard to see the things that interest Henry. But he does have interests. He doesn't wear them on his sleeve, but he does have them. There are certain things, objects, scenarios and stories that catch his imagination."

Henry often spent his weekends scavenging about the town; he walked down alleyways, investigating the objects on display in shop windows, and the ribboning network of paths around the town church and its graveyard. Over Christmas, he noticed that the brewery erected a small nativity scene on the manicured lawn outside the modern block of offices annexed to the original nineteenth century limestone building. Every time he walked past the scene, he noticed something new about the protagonists: one of the magi had lost both ears and the legs of the lamb standing adjacent to the cradle had been recreated with a skein of wire and crude patches of cotton wool. Henry never lingered at the scene; he cast covert glances at the botched artwork, assembling a record of its amateurish creation.

Henry would sometimes sit watchfully on the benches in the high-street, like a Mediterranean widow. He would see an old man frequently with a vaudevillian walk and an aluminium walking stick hobble intently along the pavement. The man scuttled quickly with a slight limp as though he was forever in a hurry. He wore thick-lens glasses that distorted his eyes. The man once tripped directly in front of Henry and tumbled to the floor with a disjointed clatter. Henry rushed to his aid as the man struggled about on the paving stones, arms and legs robbed of their intended function, like a woodlouse rolled onto its back. Henry saw that the man's facial expression was no more taciturn; he had a facial wince and his eyes raced. The way the man looked at Henry – he could clearly not make out who was helping him – led Henry to think that the man was partially blind. He saw the man many other times, walking around the town and on the bus, but the man had clearly never acknowledged Henry. The man, Henry decided, lived in a state of permanent anxiety; into the space occupied by his defective sight, Henry thought he projected his most internal fears. He was not in a hurry to reach anywhere but was forever escaping his runaway imagination.

Henry followed his observations; he let them pull him in different directions, as though there was an unseen continuity between them leading him towards the larger life of the town. He once decided to follow the man with the aluminium walking stick to see where he might take him. He saw him alight from the bus outside the bank on the corner of Wallace Roebuck Street and hurtle along, dodging pensioners, parking meters and miscreant children. He weaved between some parked cars, across the road and passed two smokers standing outside the battered warmth of the chip shop. The man followed the curve of the road until he found the entrance to the public library. He climbed the stairs, and disappeared through the sliding doors, passed the plaque dedicated to the philanthropic will of the nineteenth century industrialist and founder of the Beckthorpe Quarry who had established the building in the 1860s. Henry waited a moment, pacing about like a delinquent undecided on a course of socially unacceptable behaviour; and then he followed the man into the library.

He caught sight of the aluminium walking stick propped up against one of the long wooden reading benches at the far end of the rectangular reading room. The man had taken a seat in a comfortable, leather-cushioned chair. He was not reading or perusing the shelves. He leaned back in the chair, breathing heavily. His face was so contorted by urgency and worry, that it was hard to characterise the change in his expression; but Henry thought a smothered and half-formed look of relief was fighting for life through the man's features. The man appeared to see the library as a place of respite, a refuge from the uncertainty and danger of public spaces. In the library, he could, to an extent, recover some of the confidence his impaired vision had stolen. He settled awkwardly in his chair and, in a sudden fluster of unspent energy, reached into the inside pocket of his watercolour-grey overcoat. From here, he produced a semi-circular purse, bound by a single piece of string. He placed the purse repulsively on the wooden bench, watched it for a moment, and then reached out, in a gesture of anointment, to cover it with the palm of his hand. In this eccentric pose, he turned sharply to spy on a woman at the opposite end of the bench, reading thoughtfully from one of the library's archival tomes.

Henry's eyes flitted between the two characters at opposite ends of the reading bench. His interest in the woman was, at first, governed by the interest of the man with the aluminium walking stick; he wanted to know why she, of all people, had caught his attention. Did he think she was a threat to the strange protection he offered his purse? Or did he know her? The more Henry passed between the man and the woman, however, the more the centre of his interest shifted. Each time he looked at the woman, he seemed to notice something more about her; the details of her pose and the simple act of reading unfolded like words on a page. The woman could have been no younger than forty, but her face was young and impressionable. She was slumped softly into her chair, leaning slightly to one side, her body malleable enough to find comfort in any number of different arrangements. She had tucked the left lock of her hair behind her ear, and left the right parting to hang free with the gradient of her posture. Her shoulders were arched over the desk and her chest effused from her low-cut dress under the support of her left arm. He followed the dark line of her cleavage up to her hanging point of her chin, the spherical blush of her cheeks, and the hard sheen of her forehead. Her head slumbered from her shoulders.

The woman read with a lazy, sexual elegance; she might easily have held a cigarette issuing long tendrils of smoke at arm's length or a glass of white wine. Her body and her sexuality were not guarded or even considered; they subsisted around her, growing old with increasing insouciance.

Henry did not know how long exactly he sat staring at the woman; he had become preoccupied with her, and with a need to trace the details of his interest, to collate an inventory of the moment and her place in it. She interrupted his observations in a neat series of movements, through which she engineered her escape from the library. She reached down to pick up her bag, slid out from the bench, pulled her coat from the back of the chair, and walked unassumingly from her leisurely office.

He looked at her vacated seat, breathing the scent of her recent presence. He chased his peripheral vision to the opposite end of the bench, where he saw that the man with the aluminium walking stick had also disappeared. His trail had reached a dead-end, and for a moment, he leaned back in his chair to the let the impressions of the two characters he had watched closely slip further into his memory.

He caught sight of the volume the woman had been reading, still open on the bench. He looked around cautiously, stood up and approached the bench. The volume contained press cuttings. He began to read:

Burton ings drowning
The body of a fifty year-old woman from Riley Hutton has been recovered at Burton ings, five miles south of the town. Alice Hardcastle, a widow and lifelong resident of the town who had long been a familiar face to many of the town citizens, had not been reported missing. Her tragic and untimely death came at the height of a muscular illness from which it is believed she had been suffering for some years.

The body was found by farm bailiff, Stuart Granger from Sutton Beech farm, who caught sight of the body in the early hours of Thursday morning. Mr Granger records that he saw 'an indistinct object washed up by the ings at around six in the morning'. Upon closer examination Mr Granger identified the object as a body and notified the public authorities, who, acting on the notification, rescued the body and started a formal process of identification. Police authorities and the preliminary findings of the coroner suggest that Mrs Hardcastle had been in the water for several days.

It is presumed that the cause of death was drowning, though details of the coroner's report have been withheld pending further investigation. Mrs Hardcastle had been diagnosed with a degenerative muscular disorder five years previously.

Police-Constable Stevenson, among the first to arrive at the scene after the authorities had received notification, said:

'We do not know the facts in this case, but it is conceivable that it was an accident. Mrs Hardcastle did not have full control of her body and, if it were possible for her to have walked to the river at all, she may well have tripped, slipped or lost control of her bearing at a hazardous point along the river's edge. We are not in a position to confirm this and we shall continue to examine the case for further information.'

Mrs Hardcastle is not survived by any family; her husband died shortly after the Great War, and she had no children. A neighbour said that she would be sorely missed and that she had always shown consideration and care for those in the town community.

V

The sound caught up with her at unlikely times. If she were travelling on the bus, trying hard to hold her breath to prevent the invasion of stuffy air uncomfortably redolent of bodily fluids, she would give it some thought. Or if she were passing the colourful parade of stationary lorries in the lorry park at the rear of the brewery, she would begin to piece together the first fragments of an interpretation. These thoughts occurred rarely, if ever, in her flat.

Lena produced a diagram of the apartment building from which she hoped to build up a better understanding. She created boxes that represented each flat in the building and entered the noises and disturbances, or even the routine footsteps and flushing, that came from each one. Her hope was to identify the location of each sound so that she might visualise the patterns that linked them together; but her efforts became convoluted and self-subverting. She got lost in the smallest details, like the colour of her neighbour's cardigans and Mrs Wolf's unusual collection of Victorian culinary utensils.

Lena asked Mark and Lucinda about the sound in the building one Sunday afternoon as they walked by the river on their way to a small cupboard-sized pub in a village south of the town. They claimed that they had never noticed it; but this struck Lena as no surprise given that they were usually making their voices hoarse whenever the strange chorus of sound erupted throughout the building.

"What do you hear?" asked Mark, "A ticking sound?"

"Yes, something like a ticking sound."

"For how long have you heard this ticking sound?"

"I don't know; a few weeks or a month maybe."

"You don't have one of those old-fashioned cooking timers?"

"No."

"Or a metronome?"

Lena trailed behind her friends for a while that afternoon as her eyes scanned the flat floodplain and the snaking meanders of the river. A perimeter of debris — wood, leaves, and an assortment of non-degradable materials — marked out the extent of a recent flood. A softened afternoon light lit up the stretch of featureless wetlands; a small broken jetty protruded into a triangular confluence where a beck met the Cald. On some Sunday afternoons, solitary fisherman sat wishfully on a small beach of wet sand, pooling their luck from the sedimentary deep.

Lena's thoughts about the noise gathered pace in these moments; they were stirred up into a semi-recognisable shape. But the geometry of the shape was difficult to pin down. The sound, she thought, was educational. The patterns she could begin to detect when she reflected on the noise implied the idea of a lesson, or imparted knowledge from which the soundscape of her building took its cue. Whenever the noise began, the activities and behaviour of the building and its inhabitants took a new direction, governed, or in some sense, influenced by the noise.

Pipes clattered, central heating choked and spluttered, small insects climbed out from ageing, overlooked interstices, and a mood descended on the building, a mood of pent-up tension on the point of vocalising an indescribable anger and frustration. This anger, which at other times seemed to have splintered throughout the unseen corners of the building and to live among the settled motes of dust, was roused and rallied. It found, or *learned*, a cohesion that it otherwise lacked.

Her efforts to understand, though tucked away vaguely at the back of her mind, continued. She composed numerous notes, written on scraps of paper, like forgotten shopping lists stuffed into her trouser pockets or folded into the innermost corners of her handbag. She drew several diagrams. She produced interactive models of behaviour from bits of moulding fruit. She lingered on the streets outside the house in search of any signs from the floors above.

In one of her experiments, she set an old recorder running once the mechanical rhythm of the ticking began. She played the content of it back once the noise had stopped, but she could only hear the empty crackle of static. She fast-forwarded, hoping that she might not have started recording from the beginning. Three-quarters of the way through she chanced upon the final phonics of a male voice; the word pronounced, sounded like '...ocked'. It took her some time, but she soon found the beginning of the captured voice. It did not say much, and the tonality and intention of the words were polite, gentle and unassuming, declared more as a wish than the instruction it at first suggested.

"Please, there is no need to keep your door locked," the voice said simply.

VI

Henry revisited the library many times, where he discovered similar stories filed away in the archives. It slotted into his routine; he discovered the right journey, the right hour and the right desk for his research. He soon came to realise that the library was at its quietest very early on a Saturday morning. He formed the habit of going to bed early on a Friday night after work, getting up at around seven, and then visiting *The Dirty Café* to pick up a bacon and sausage butty – with brown sauce – before traipsing across the chipped concrete of the central car park, passed the assembling trestle tables and itinerant gazebos of the market.

Henry, like the old man with the aluminium walking stick, discovered safety and comfort in the library. The rectangular reading room was on the first floor. A vernal morning light brought in through the high rose windows above the bookcases descended on the stillness of the room. At this hour of the day, at this time of the year, with the light waking on the books, the library became a place on the verge of discovery. There was no academic mahogany, nor anything faintly ornate about the reading room; it felt the under-nourishment of public funds. The books were all bound with decaying laminate covers and the two computers looked like they had been rushed through accident and emergency.

Henry always sat in the same corner at the furthest point from the reception desk. The hard copies of the local newspaper – those that were not microfiched – were kept in large bound volumes on the wall adjacent to his elected desk. Two long pendant fixtures hung above each bench projecting pools of light designated for reading, which, in juxtaposition with the settled, sepia-grey that shaded the reversed space of the lit area, created a half-living chiaroscuro. Henry liked to lean carefully into the edge of this theatre of light, in the centre of which he had splayed out one of the enormous volumes. From this spectator spot, he nosed through the fine-leaded print.

In frequent breaks from his research, Henry formed a relationship with the drinks machine plugged into the wall to the rear of the landing area at the top of the main staircase. He always punched in the same number – tea with milk – and waited as it prised the drink forcefully from its gut. The mechanical bronchitis that came from the machine sounded like a device of medieval torture, and seemed to require an energy out of all proportion with the quality of the chemical intoxicant it produced. Between his reflections on the history of unfortunates drowned in the river – who had by this time become the victims of murder – he supped cautiously over the rim of his cup, examining the public notice board for regional events, groups and other social activities.

The breaks in his routine contributed to the excitement of his enterprise. They provided moments in which he could pause to think about his discoveries; they gave him the opportunity to 'see' what he was doing and to extract from it a rush of excitement. He enjoyed wrapping his hands around the warm paper cup filled with an approximate brew, and leaning back against the radiator that throbbed hard to heat the high-ceilinged room and cold, banausic home for public knowledge.

Henry was not, in this sense, pursuing this interest in an entirely scientific way. He had no trance-like fixation with a goal, the mathematical calculations for the achievement of which had only to be worked through with appropriate rigour and method. He could feel the magnetic pull of his research, as though it was waiting to swallow him whole.

Henry thought that, to the original readers of each story he discovered, any overarching pattern would not have been obvious. The articles might have elicited feelings of shock, sympathy for the victim, or alarm but the time span of the incidents made it less likely that the respective readers would have seen any connection. Much less would it have suggested to these readers that the bodies pulled from the river had been murdered. The conclusion that they had been murdered by the same person would have been still less probable. But to Henry, who looked back on these articles from a broader vantage point, who had studied the details and the victims, and who had arranged and rearranged the facts to explore all the avenues of interpretation and the logic on which each depended, the connection was, if not clear, then at least possible.

A single fact, which he found through a passing reference to the original 1918 murder in a book about the history of the brewery, crystallised his view and shed light on the parallels between the different stories. He had noticed that almost all the victims he had studied had, in the period immediately preceding their death, suffered some form of misfortune, physical or psychological distress or despair, or simply that they had lost the patronage of good luck. Alice Hardcastle, the subject of the first article to have awakened his curiosity, had suffered from a form of congenital myopathy. A boy found in the river in the late 1940s experienced a period of near psychotic behaviour before the river accommodated his unrest – he had first tried to stab a fellow student at his school and then made an abortive attempt to hang himself. A man discovered wrapped around some driftwood on the weir close to the farming hamlet, Ashton Prior, in 1964, had been the owner of a small printing firm until it went bankrupt two weeks before his disappearance.

A strange case, and one that conformed to the pattern of dissolution preceding disappearance, set these articles in a broader context: in 1980, the bodies of two twin sisters, who lived in Salford had disappeared and were found a week later just outside the town close to the point at which the river joined the Ouse. The twins had run away together from their adopted home in Salford; the article speculated that this was for reasons of domestic abuse. The reference in the book about the history of the brewery, which Henry encountered with the clammy aftertaste of brown sauce still in his throat, explained that the policeman's wife had been pregnant with twins.

Henry's thoughts and researches, his steady accumulation of evidence, examined to winnow out the chaff from the grain, moved in a new direction. His copious notes and records of fact, the premises he had collected over weeks became inflected with speculations to form a complete syllogism.

He began re-reading. He hunted out the articles he had already read and went through them again. He found no new fragments of fact, and though there were pieces of information he had overlooked the first time around, there was nothing to add to the bare bones of each narrative. But, in each case, he read in a different way or from a different perspective; where his initial researches had constituted an exhausting piece-by-piece, step-by-step, moment-by-moment ascent, he was now looking down panoramically on the extracts from each life, able to cross-reference and compare the details. And this perspective did not complete the puzzle; the more he interrogated the facts, the more he threaded the continuities and sectioned off the discontinuities, the more open-ended the logical implications of his research became. The findings were not closed and discrete; they grew exponentially.

The murder — the original 1918 murder — was, he decided, alive. It was in motion, continually re-enacted through the lives of people in the town who had fallen foul of fortune. It was no longer just an historical murder but a trans-historical murder. He had first been struck by the slender similarity between the appearance of each body in the river and the fact that the policeman's wife had also been discovered there. That the policeman's wife had been pregnant with twins and a pair of twins had disappeared in 1980 only to be found in the river had consolidated this similarity. That some reports – he could only find occasional references – recorded injuries to the stomachs of some bodies compounded his curiosity. The owner of the printing firm found in the river at Ashton Prior weir had been pulled from the water with, in the words of the article, 'a punctured stomach'. He discovered a scare-mongering article about the rise in alcohol consumption and the dangers it entailed, which referred to a thirty year-old brewery administrator called Philip Wilmslow who was believed to have fallen in the river only a few years previously after a night out drinking, but who was unable to extricate himself from the water. To reinforce the horror, the article added the detail that the victim had suffered 'severe damage to the midriff'. (This was the only reference he could find to this particular incident.) Only a few years into the new millennium, a girl from eastern Europe, who had worked as a prostitute, was pulled from the river with five 'small holes' in her lower abdomen.

The last case put the others in the same broader context and made him want to know more about the wounds. The figure of five wounds in the case of the eastern European girl resonated with him; and when he returned to the details of the 1918 murder he remembered that the policeman was alleged to have stabbed his wife five times.

Henry was intrigued by the incongruity of interpretation between his embryonic big-picture extrapolation and the glosses of interpretation tacked on suggestively by the reporters coining the opportunity for (sometimes moralising, sometimes philosophical) speculation. Each article seemed to carry the baggage of the time in which the event occurred, and each writer had interpreted the events strictly within the limits of this hermeneutic frame. In all cases, the writers had learned to do this with calculated discretion aware of taking too much from the available facts. The article about the eastern European girl played on the dangers of immigration by quoting a Home Office estimate of illegal immigrants adjacent to a more general statement about the spread of sex trafficking and its evasive but hand-holding twin, violent crime. The piece about the printer seized on the opportunity to headline a campaign of the moment – directed at the owner of the brewery and much of the land in and around the town – petitioning against the improper maintenance of public footpaths. The story about the twins from Salford, in a short but pointed final paragraph, noted that there had been at least four other prominent cases of young girls disappearing in the years leading up to the case that had cast a spotlight on 'known pederasts'. Though murder was sometimes implicit, as in this last case and the case of the eastern European girl, it was explained by feasible precedents. But in many cases, the deaths were often conjectured variously as accidents or, in some cases, suicides.

These interpretations snatched hurriedly and extemporarily in the knockabout heat of press rooms from established points of view were, in their context, if not well-founded then inductively possible. Henry reasoned that the reporters on each of these cases were only making the most of the facts that were available. It could never fall within their remit to research the kind of landscape comparison that he had undertaken.

In an effort to represent the theory that was forming in his mind, he imagined that each article, each interpretation, was a circle and the facts that informed the articles were its centre. The length of the radius between the centre and the edge of the circle was the same for all the articles. But *his* interpretation was like an 'outer' circle drawn around these 'inner' circles, so that he could see each one in the context of a greater radius from the truth at its centre.

These concentric circles of interpretation created a dual perspective from which to look at the different events. To the writers of each article the deaths made sense as, for example, an outcome of subterranean crime or the debilitating effects of a muscular disease. But from Henry's outer circle of interpretation, all could be explained as recurrences of the policeman who murdered his wife in 1918. Each death was a way of retelling or reliving the same horrific event.

But Henry's model of two concentric circles of interpretation and a 'dual perspective' was misleading. It was misleading for the simple reason that he could not make sense of it. If it were true that the history of disappearances in the town were instantiations of the same historical murder, the 'perspective' from which each event could be understood in this way was unthinkable. It defied the a priori logic of time. According to his model, it implied the idea of not another circle outside his own in the context of which everything made sense, but an infinite expanse of concentric circles and an infinite number of perspectives, regressing to simple absurdity.

Through this speculative theorising conducted in dimly lit rooms with asbestos warning stickers on the walls, he thought he could detect the inner workings of the murder, its nature and geometry. The violent act of 1918 was not only an act of physical destruction but an unravelling and trouncing of the mind. It confounded not the evidence that informed any given interpretation but the very *act* of interpretation.

But it did not – or would not – stop there. That the murder confounded the conditions for interpretation meant that all acts of interpretation – including those found in the articles he had studied, his piecemeal theory, even the studious thoughts he hurled fitfully from his brain each time he approached the subject – worked *against* their objective. They limited the murder and therefore created a barrier between the student and the object of study. If he had begun to discern the skeleton of the murder through his research, the interpretations that collected around it, including his own, were the flesh and blood and the form of subsistence on which it remained fugitive. It had been sprinkled here and there, smuggled into variegated circumstances at different points in history; and the people who encountered its repetitions concealed the murder through their encounters, through the meaning they gave to the events. This meant that it would necessarily evade detection. 'The murder attributed to paedophilia', 'the drowning explained by drunkenness', 'the prostitute caught up in the world of organised crime' were all trip switches, coils, racks and pinions that formed a machinery of defence. The murder was a lucent half-formed phantom, disguised in the tawdry town-wear of time.

Henry tossed and turned over the murder. It even intruded on his meditative moments at the coffee machine; where he had previously punched in numbers in a perfunctory fashion, now he looked over the keypad as though even this simple activity involved complex permutations of thought. He no longer leaned against the radiator, soaking up the combined warmth of the bars and the industry of his study; instead he paced about the landing area enacting his intellectual unrest. He even started to forge peculiar connections between his state of mind and his movements. He speculated that his mind was forcing his body to act and conjectured that a physical vestige of the problem over which he fretted might be obvious in his movements. Perhaps he was walking in codified shapes that embodied the circuitous logic of the murder. Perhaps his interest in certain words on the public notice board – 'ornithological', 'playgroup', 'coloratura' – were reflections of an unconscious grasp of the issue. Perhaps, he thought, the murder was living through him, flourishing and breathing through the very act of study. He slit the wrapper on a chocolate bar, ground the lactic cocoa between his molars and fixed his eyes on the objects and spaces before him, like Neanderthal man struggling to make the connection between his growling stomach, the club in his hand, and the feast of meat grazing before him in a primordial meadow.

At his desk once more, Henry began sentences with no end or which trailed off with an unsatisfactory and unmarked ellipsis. He pictorialised the problem in pie charts and scatter diagrams that he could not complete and which left him doodling in the margins. He wanted to know more about the architecture and mechanics of the murder. Was each incident linear and temporal? Was each murder contrived spontaneously as a suitable victim became available? Was the murderer cleverly concealed, spying on the town and waiting to react? Henry did not think so. He preferred a different model of explanation. Each murder was, he thought, a logical variant on the original. The first murder was an analytical container for the subsequent murders; it made possible every ensuing repetition, so that the act was a continuous and complete operation traceable back to origins. The repetitions were pieces or instances of the full historical event.

If this were the case, then the historical examples Henry had exhumed might be only the tip of the iceberg; and his theory was, itself, only an intimation of the real events. Other aspects of the murder – including lesser details such as its circumstance, motive, means and opportunity – might have been revealed, or might yet be revealed, in other examples from the town's history and future. Even the smallest and most unlikely details from the town might have a dual (or multiple) significance: a particular bench, stretches of pathway around the town, and the facade of certain shops, might, at once, appear as everything they at first seemed, and yet might be a granular pixel part of a cruel but coherent whole.

But it was a clear corollary of Henry's reasoning that the story of the murder could never be told. The murder had been plotted and premeditated to ensure it could never be told. To study the murder, to tell its story, only created yet another angle, yet another testimony among the torpid layers of testimony. If people stopped writing about it, if people were disinterested, if *he* were disinterested, if the mind stopped functioning, then the murder might be grasped; it was as though the instinctive reactions of the human psyche were complicit with the criminal act and that the two were inextricably bound to each other. The murder relied on *mis*-understanding as a condition of all thought and implicitly mocked the mind in all its feeble, logical fumbling and feckless attributions of meaning.

Henry's energies began to wane. And in-between his productive bursts of work, he thought, parenthetically, about the point of his research. He could never hope to apprehend the murderer ('apprehension' had gone the same way as 'comprehension'). He was not sure yet where his own trail would lead him or where it might lead the person following in his stead.

But the nature of the murder unpacked this new angle of reflection. The murder stood at an absolute, or an infinite, distance from intuition and common sense. To even attempt an understanding of what was at work in the town, however partial and fragmented, meant moving in the same direction *away* from intuition and common sense. And even now he realised that his own rheumy-eyed thoughts meant that *he* was speaking the language of the murderer. He was speaking, writing, thinking, and living from a perspective increasingly removed the accepted idioms of common sense, one that intimated the broader, near unfathomable, life of the murder. His research was not examining the crime objectively; it was an instrument of seduction inviting him into the fold of an arcane madness; and it seemed to follow logically that someone would at some point be looking down at his face in the paper and reading into the now considerably more terse and sensationalist print, the details of *his* disappearance.

Robert Stewart

The terrier

I

If ever Lena cleaned the rooms of her flat, she cleaned to impress. Or, at least, she cleaned to avoid a bad impression. Where the situation could go either way she erred on the side of caution. Even with the right motivation her efforts were partial at best. She always homed in on the most prominent objects, like the table, her shelves, and the television. She would give them a quick once over and any other clutter in the room she shovelled away into corners, in drawers, under sofas or beds. Lena's flat was a bulky woman squeezed into a tight-fitting corset and made-up for a special occasion.

Richard Terrier was the occasion. The Terrier languished on Lena's couch in a linen jacket, jeans and a 'What's wrong with Tofu?' t-shirt. His long hair had enjoyed some serious grooming. He looked perky and chirpy sitting on Lena's sofa; his face was bursting with the freshness of an Amazonian rain forest. Lena noticed the way his trousers hugged his legs; they matched perfectly the architecture of his lower body as though they were just an extension of his natural shape and form. When he leaned back on the sofa, his shoulders were squared and upright. The long hair, to her mind, signalled a controlled rebellion; this was a person who knew both how to please and, consequently, how to subvert.

She peered out from the kitchen at him just to take in the spectacle. He was reading from a music magazine when he looked up at her and smiled.

"Would you like some wine?" she asked.

"Yes, I could stomach a glass of vino," he said with a smile.

"Okay," she said and disappeared back into the kitchen.

Lena was whipping up a Chinese.

She had bought several bottles of wine earlier in the day. She reached into a cupboard and grabbed one indiscriminately. She rooted around for some glasses and placed them on her small kitchen table.

The Terrier appeared in the doorway. He shifted his weight from one foot to the other.

"Can I help?" he asked.

Lena screwed into the cork of the wine bottle firmly. She tried to pull the cork from the bottle but it was stuck.

"Could you have a go?" she asked, handing him the bottle.

"Sure."

The Terrier stepped up to the task heroically. He pulled at the cork and dislodged it partially. He placed the bottle between his thighs and, straining, he pulled the cork free from the bottle.

Lena noticed he seemed to have strong thighs. She wondered if he played a lot of football or rugby. If he did, she wondered if his hair got in the way or if opponents would sometimes cheat by giving his hair a discreet yank when the referee wasn't looking.

"I have quite strong thighs as well," she said.

The Terrier laughed.

"I once knew a guy who was mad about music. He managed to get a job as a music journalist for a time. In London. And he listened to so many CDs, he got so many free promos that in the end he just couldn't stand it anymore. He got sick of it. Does that not happen to you? After you have cooked your five hundredth steak and kidney pie or whatever, don't you just want to scream?"

Lena ran her fingers through her hair and tied it back with a band, before leaning over her wok to check if the groundnut oil had started to spit.

"Well it's a job," she replied as though she was being interviewed. "I probably wouldn't cook as much if I didn't have to. But variety is the spice of life; I cook different things and I look for different recipes. I haven't got bored yet. It's a bit different, but I have met loads of chefs who say that they cook so much that they very often don't feel hungry. You know, like if you are feeling hungry and you do some exercise your hunger goes away? They say it's a bit like that. Imagine that though; it must be awful – you can't enjoy all the tasty things you have created. I'm lucky though. I don't have that problem. I'm always hungry."

"'You can always make room for a current bun,' – that's what my granny said. She came from a poor background."

"We live in a different age. These days she would have said 'You can always make room for some raspberry panna cotta.'"

Tomas handed her a glass of wine. Lena looked at her wok objectively.

"There's something very simple about food. I am a very simple person."

The Terrier didn't quite know what to say so he looked over Lena's ingredients, collected in little bowls on the side. He saw some garlic, root ginger, chestnut mushrooms, spring onions, a bottle of rice wine, some Soy sauce and a sieve full of egg noodles draining in the sink.

"Are you hungry?" she asked.

"A bit."

"Have you had any lunch today?"

"I ate an apple and an orange."

"That's all?"

"Yes."

"You must be hungry?"

"Quite hungry."

"You should eat. You lose your strength if you don't eat. Should I start cooking now, do you think?"

She took a sip from her wine, and looked out of the glass at the Terrier as she drank.

"I can wait. Sometimes I only get hungry when I start eating. When I've starved myself, I can go for hours."

"I'm not like that. I need food."

"Uh huh."

Lena took another sip from her wine. She searched the Terrier for a subject of conversation, for something about his person which interested her. It was the same look she gave to a meal before she tucked in. She was examining, sniffing and approving. It was her ritual of the appetite.

"I have heard some people say that there is a close connection between food and sex."

Though he had seen it coming, the Terrier looked slightly unsettled. He stood still for the first time, and looked back at Lena as boldly as he knew how.

"Really," he said.

"Because both are about the body. So people who like food like sex. I like food."

"I see."

"I once went out with a boy when I was fifteen," she continued, "who couldn't always control himself. Sometimes, if we kissed for about five minutes, he would come in his trousers. I didn't touch him. I didn't even give him a trouser-fondle. The first time it happened, I didn't know what was wrong. He would make this feeble little whimper in his throat and then look down at the floor, embarrassed. It took me a long time to realise what was going on. When I finally got it, I remember I just laughed for ages. From then on, I started to touch him and I let him touch me. He came even quicker then. He had a very healthy appetite."

"Well," said the Terrier, "I'm sure you are right; food is pretty important."

"Are you sure you're not hungry?"

"Like I say, once I start nibbling, I tend to get hungry."

"Perhaps you would like something to nibble."

A large bubble of boiling groundnut oil popped, spraying Lena's right arm with several droplets. She flinched slightly, but treated the attack as a prompt to start cooking. She had learned over time that receiving burns was an essential part of cooking; if at the end of a shift, she did not have at least one fresh burn, she felt she had not been working hard enough.

Lena scraped some slices of marinated chicken breast and some bacon into the wok; a searing and sibilant conflict began to take place and a sprinkle of oil splashed against the edges and over its side. She shovelled the meat around the wok, encouraging the volatile oil and sending up a constant vapour of steam from the juices of the meat.

"You know, you have just given me a thought. I don't want to bore you, but can I tell you about my week?"

"Was it exciting?"

"Yes, I had an interesting week. I run this ... it's sort of like a monthly event to promote individual talents. It started out as a music thing. I got together with some friends who thought that there wasn't enough diversity in the music scene. You know, you get a lot of certain types of music but not a real diversity of types; I mean, like, world types. So once a month, we have a venue and loads of different bands and groups come along and they get their fifteen minutes. The idea was to promote a sort of awareness of different art forms and an appreciation of different cultural forms of expression, you know. But it just grew. I started doing a similar thing but with fashions; so we would look at things like colour codes and how different cultures look at different fashions; someone else has done literature and films. This week I decided that the theme was going to be green; so we, like, looked at the different ways in which countries and fashions have made use of green. It was freaky some of it. We were garlanded in green.

'But I was thinking, you know, one or two people I have spoken to have mentioned doing something with food and stuff; you know, they said we should do the same thing but with food. We haven't got around to it yet, but it would be good to get started. You would definitely be able to come up with some stuff."

Lena's mind was still on sex.

"I suppose I could make some soup or something. What sort of thing would it be? Vegetables?"

"It could be anything. Just anything that you like."

"I like everything."

Lena imagined sitting alone in a parish hall on a wet weekend at a stall with a display of cooked meats and an ox turning on a spit as ethnic types walked by disapprovingly in the direction of another stall promoting Mediterranean root vegetables and fungi.

"It's just so that people are more aware of what's out there. I mean you must know loads of different dishes. I mean when I grew up I ate boiled fish and bangers and mash. I had curry and Chinese and stuff but there's so much more to be discovered. Don't you reckon?"

"What? Like other countries?"

"Yeah. Yeah, other countries."

"I like bangers and mash."

"Yeah, well that's cool, you know."

"And gravy. With onions, mushrooms ... and liver."

"Well for someone who has never eaten gravy before, you could be their guide."

"Well, I like all foods from everywhere. I like sushi."

"We gotta get down together to the tune of the global funk y'all!" said the Terrier, feigning a bad accent.

Thoughtfulness punctuated the conversation.

Lena started to remove the chunks of meat from the wok. She wondered if she had embarrassed the Terrier by talking about sex.

"But, I mean, there's a serious point, you know. People have to learn to live together. We've got to *ed-u-cate*."

"I'll give it some thought."

Lena replenished the groundnut oil in the wok and threw in some chopped garlic.

"Should I tell you about my week?"

"Has it been exciting?"

"Not very long ago, someone I met in the pub disappeared. He lived in the town. I had never met him before. But apparently he lived on the edge of the town in a bungalow. So he disappeared. No-one has seen him since."

"No-one knows what might have happened to him?"

"Not many people knew him – I didn't know him – so I'm not sure if anyone really cares. But here is the thing: when I talked to him in the pub, he lied to me: he told me he worked as a journalist, when he worked in the post office; he told me a made-up story about a Scottish midget; he lied about his name – he said he was called Henry when his real name was Andrew. And he told me a story about a policeman who murdered his wife in the town sometime in the early twentieth century. But the strange thing is, you see, this week … this week, you see, my uncle told me that the story about the policeman is true."

"The one who murdered his wife?"

"And that's not the end of it either. No. You see, my uncle says that since the policeman murdered his wife there has been a *history* of people disappearing in this town."

Lena was, by now, adding ingredients to the wok frantically; she threw in the root ginger, some mangetout, the chopped chestnut mushrooms. The wok had become a hive of activity. Finally she added the egg noodles she had left to drain.

"There were some twins and a woman with some sort of muscle problem who went missing, and some other people as well. So this has been going on since the 1910s. And then this person I met in the pub the other day goes missing. So now I am thinking that he is just one more in the long history of people who have disappeared in this town. And this is the thing: all of these people that have disappeared – this is what my uncle told me – were found eventually in the river. They were found dead in the river."

"How terrible."

"And do you know that the person I met in the pub talked – when he talked about it, he sort of sounded like he was joking – he talked all the time about the river. He went on about it. He went on about the power of the river and how a white whale had got caught in the river in the nineteenth century."

"A whale?"

"A white whale. It's weird."

"Yes."

The Terrier looked troubled.

"Well your week has certainly been more interesting than mine."

"It's strange really to look back at it, but yes, I think you are right. Though 'interesting' isn't really the right word."

Lena splashed the mixture in her wok with rice wine, some Soy sauce and sesame oil. She threw the cooked meat and their juices back into the wok and continued to stir.

II

Lena and the Terrier were sitting down together at the table in Lena's front room. They both shovelled in mouthfuls of food. The Terrier had been right, she thought; once he got a taste for something, he pulled out the stops. He was a noisy eater. He breathed heavily. He chomped and slurped.

"This is very good," he said, with his mouth half full.

"Thanks."

"You're a very good cook."

"You have very good shoulders," said Lena, eyeing the Terrier the same face full of fun.

"How did you make that connection?"

"I was returning the compliment. You have nice shoulders."

Lena kept herself amused by imagining the Terrier seated before her naked with a trail of egg noodle disappearing into his chomping hole. She was still in the process of deciding whether or not he still had his underpants on, or if he was fully in the buff.

"You seem to have found your hunger," she said.

"Yes; it's delicious."

"I see what you mean."

"I'm sorry?"

"I see what you mean about your hunger. It seems to pick up the more you eat."

"Particularly when I haven't eaten much all day. And the food is good."

"I'm pretty hungry as well."

"Are we talking about food or sex now?"

"Both."

Lena could see no reason to keep it secret.

"Just so long as we know."

"Would you like some more wine?" she asked, "But like I've said there is a connection; when I was in Holland a girlfriend – I think she may have made the story up – but there was a girlfriend of mine who told me a story about a man with a fetish. It was all about onions. He would go out with girls for weeks; he would even sleep with them without showing any signs of sexual misbehaviour, but his only motivation, the goal that obsessed him, was that at some point in the relationship he would introduce onions."

"What do you mean?"

"He wanted to associate an onion with the girl or the other way around (I can't remember) – anyway, he wanted there to be some connection. And then once he had made the connection, he would use the onion privately, and before the onion could rot, he would cook it and eat it."

"You know some weird stuff."

"It was a bit like the way men get a thing about women's underwear. But with food. Sometimes, if he could get the girl to play along, he would ask her to sit naked as she held onions while he touched himself."

"Right," said the Terrier seriously.

"So, you see, sometimes there is a very direct connection between food and sex. They are both very sensual things."

Lena had decided by now that the Terrier in her mind's eye was definitely not wearing underpants.

"Have you ever touched yourself over an onion? Or a potato? Or a stick of broccoli?" she asked mischievously.

"No."

The Terrier was looking like he might crumble. His eating had slowed up. He tried to put the same brave face on the situation, answering Lena's questions directly without flinching. But his face turned a flashlight pink. Irritation cut a crease in his forehead. He looked mildly frustrated with Lena, as though all her talk of fetishes had been meant to humiliate him.

"It's just silly," she said, conscious of his souring mood.

"Yes, I suppose."

Lena did what she always did in awkward moments: she looked to her family.

"Do your family live near here?" she asked.

"No, my family live in Bristol. I went to university in Leeds."

"I never went to university. Even if I had gone knocking at their door, they would have cast me out like ... like a swineherd. They would have said 'Go live with the swineherd Lena, where you belong! Go learn about meat and seasoning! Go learn how to flame-grill a chicken!"

"What do students know? So much of student life is so noisy. Sometimes you just want to take a back seat. Sometimes you just want a bit of peace."

"Yes, sometimes."

"Didn't you say you are half Dutch?"

"My mother was Dutch. She died when I was thirteen. She had cancer. But my father grew up in the North York Moors. My father, when he was young, would sometimes go over to a place called Ravenscar on the East Coast, just north of Scarborough. He would look out to sea. He and my mother calculated that it was possible the two of them could have been looking at each other across the North Sea at the same time. That's what they liked to think anyway. When she was ill, my father would always remind her. He would bring her photographs from his childhood. But it always upset her. My father would make up stupid stories about how he was so miserable before he met my mother. He said he was an angry stone-kicker who only grunted at the world and sighed a lot. At that time, there was a coastal railway in Ravenscar. He would tell my mother that he would keep looking out to sea, dreaming about his future love, until a train tooted through a tunnel. Then he would sigh and turn his back on the ocean. He said it was like he knew my mother *before* he knew my mother. When he started to go on about it, my mother told him to bring in the coal."

Lena stood up and walked across the room to the bookcase. She picked up a box of matches and lit a T-light on the shelf.

"I like to light a candle sometimes, when I am remembering my mother."

She leaned back onto the sofa.

"Are you not hungry anymore?" she asked, undoing the top button of her shirt.

"Here we go."

Lena laughed.

"There's plenty more if you want some."

A slit in her dress partially exposed her right leg. She reached forward to rub at her ankle. She stroked her hand back up her leg, making the slit in her dress wider.

"You look like you want some more."

The Terrier looked like he had an appetite undecided on an object. Lena laughed again.

"I wish I had a camera for your face. It's all right," she said, standing up. "I won't bite. Well, not much."

She pulled up a chair next to him, so that they were nearly face to face. She hunched over the table and folded her arms. The combined movements lifted her chest assertively. She looked down at the Terrier's plate.

"Maybe I should feed you. Would you like me to feed you?"

Inarticulate sounds came from the Terrier's throat.

Lena picked out a noodle from his plate.

"I used to do this with friends when I was little. It was like a test to see who could go the furthest. I always won."

She held the noodle up to the Terrier's mouth.

"Open your mouth," she instructed. "You take one end."

The Terrier obeyed.

She placed one end of the noodle in his mouth and the other end in her mouth. They both sucked on the noodle, and when there was no noodle left, they kissed.

The Terrier recovered some life once they started to kiss; he cradled her head with his hand and shuffled his body closer. Lena nearly choked on some of the noodle in her mouth, and so she broke free to make some room. But the Terrier was set in motion: he leaned closer still, planting his lips around her neck. Lena, pleasantly surprised, ran one of her hands up his trouser leg.

"You might think that food, sex and my family are unrelated," she said slowly. "But in my mind they are related. If you have an appetite for food, you have an appetite for sex; and you can't have a family without sex. But that's not it completely. They are connected like that, but there is something else that brings them together. I have thought about this a lot, you see. It's what everyone calls love; and, to my mind, you see, it blossoms and blooms in different ways, like a garden full of many different varieties of flower. It is like a garden, and in this garden everything is growing and flourishing, thirsting after something, whether its food, sex, people or whatever."

"Uh huh," said the Terrier, as he peeled her shirt from her shoulder.

Lena kissed him on the cheek and undid the fly on his trousers.

"Do you know, when I was only about seventeen, I went on a semi-nudist beach in France. I remember lying on my front in a quiet little corner of the beach with a sunhat over my head. I looked to my right and I saw that there was a boy a bit younger than me lying naked on his side with his front facing me. When I looked down at his crotch, I could see that he was aroused. He didn't even move. At first, I thought he was asleep. I couldn't tell because he had sunglasses on. I remember I wondered what he was dreaming about. But then the boy suddenly removed his sunglasses and I saw that he was looking straight at me. I don't know whether or not he could see me staring at him. It only occurred to me slowly, but I realised that it was the sight of me lying naked that had made him hard. And I remember thinking that I had some claim to his boner. It felt like it belonged to me. Nothing happened between us, but it was very erotic."

"Do you keep anything to yourself?"

"I would like to keep a boy to myself. But they always get away."

Lena smuggled her tongue inside the Terrier's head. She stood up and pulled him with her. They stumbled across the room to the sofa. Lena made a failed attempt to rip his t-shirt off. She made a slight tear in the seam underneath his armpit. The Terrier looked slightly peeved, as though she had reduced the value of the shirt. He undertook the task alone.

Lena stood over the Terrier, who leaned into the sofa, as she threw her shirt away. She unzipped her skirt and let it drop to the floor.

The Terrier followed Lena's sinuous outline in awe and fear. Lena stroked her right hand down her left arm in a gesture of false repulsion. Her movements were lackadaisical, like a carefree jazz singer moving confidently towards a show-stopping crescendo.

Lena kneeled on the couch at the Terrier's side. She loomed slightly above him, so that he had to look up to receive her affection. The Terrier flattened the palm of his hand against her breast; Lena, hurriedly and keen to encourage unbarred access to her body, undid her bra strap.

The two kissed, groped, fondled and fumbled; but, without any real warning, the Terrier suddenly withdrew all his paws from her person and looked down at the carpet disconsolately. Lena was too involved to really notice. She continued to play with his hair and kiss him. The Terrier only caught her attention by goading her away at the shoulder.

"I'm not sure about this," he said weakly.

Lena was amused by the healthy flush of red in his cheeks.

"Oh," she said. "Oh right. You don't … oh right."

"It's just … I don't know."

The Terrier shuffled into the corner of the sofa. He scratched the back of his head and looked around the room for some kind of assistance. It looked like he might say something else; he inhaled and raised his hand as though he was about to deliver a thorough explanation. But he remained silent. He made his corner on the sofa look like a temporary retreat in which no-one could look and no-one could judge.

Lena sighed and flopped back into her corner of the sofa. She poked her stomach for fun.

The Terrier had taken a troublesome journey to a land of night and shadow. His face was full of introspection. He looked serious. A frown, like the burden of original sin, spoiled his forehead, and his hair swallowed his face slowly. Soon he would be a body with a shaggy mop of hair for a head.

Lena lifted her legs onto the sofa and stretched out so that her feet rested in his lap. She jabbed his thigh with her toes.

"Richard …"

The Terrier looked at her through crestfallen eyes.

"Richard, would you like a pudding? Or a coffee? I could make some coffee."

"Yes," he croaked.

She smiled at him.

She swung her legs out of his lap and clambered across the sofa on all fours. She found a place at his side and set her head to rest on his shoulder.

She could feel the tension in his body begin to drain slowly.

"I will make some coffee in a moment," she said.

"Okay."

The two remained in this position for several minutes. Lena toyed with strands of his hair and ran her fingers up and down the length of his left forearm. She nuzzled in his neck, turning her head slowly through an angle so that she could see his expression. Her left hand strayed to his chest. She felt his breastbone with the tips of her fingers, and reached up to kiss him on the cheek.

The Terrier shuffled cautiously in his seat so that their faces might meet. The Terrier's eyes were fixed on the ground, and systematically avoided all contact with Lena's searching body and her probing hands. His head fell forward. Lena kissed him again, her lips moving closer to his. He rested his forehead against hers. Lena bit his top lip, and, slowly, full of weary grace, she clambered on top of him.

"Just think of me as a fairground ride," she said.

III

"One of the interesting things about this murder," said Tomas, "is the problem of its interpretation. I am sure that if you examined case studies, you would find that different murders have been explained in different ways. Some are committed in order to achieve an end. Politicians have been assassinated to remove an obstacle to a perceived good. Civilians are killed who stand in the way of a successful heist. Offenders are expunged to appease a group vendetta. In pre-classical times, humans were sometimes sacrificed to ensure a stable social and cosmological equilibrium. In all these cases, the murder is the means to the achievement of a goal that is desirable in the mind of the perpetrator."

Tomas and Lena were together once again. They were sitting next to each other, arranged and governed by the same balance of curiosity and knowledge. Lena was quiet and part-attentive, her mind periodically distracted by the flight of a sparrow or the sparrowing about of three young boys trying hard to graffiti the retractable metal shutter at the entrance to a warehouse on the opposite bank of the river with caricatures of male genitalia. Tomas talked with cold, confident irony, subtly aware of the sequences of thought to which he was subjecting his niece and conscious of her roving attentions. The two subjects, though still following out the same enquiry and in the same way, had changed surroundings. It was a Monday afternoon towards the end of March and they were sitting, like pensioners on a day out excited by burgeoning daffodils and the first aromatic fragrances of spring, on a bench at the edge of the riverbank as the sun wiped the sleep from the wintry landscape.

"But to arrive at any of these interpretations, the person studying the facts had available to them a set of determinate events. They had the privileged perspective of posterity. They were 'looking back' ironically and objectively at a story that had already occurred. From this objective point of view, they could unpick the details to arrive at these different conclusions. But in this case, though there is a history of events, their nature suggests that the object of study is indeterminate. I mean we are talking about a murder that is re-occurring, unbound by the conventions of time. A murderer has not been found. The case has never been closed. This suggests that the murder is not an historical murder but, on the contrary, that it is incomplete. It is a story that is still unfolding, which means that all studies of the murder are pre-emptive; they occur inside the narrative they are trying to unravel – they are like an attempt to tell a story before it is complete.

'In most murder investigations, the criminal is brought to justice either by crunching data or a lucky break, which gives the detective an advantage over the criminal. But this murder is the other way around – the murder always has the advantage because it forestalls the conditions which make possible any kind of interpretation. To think of it at all within a time frame that makes sense is necessarily a misrepresentation of it. This means that the murderer is not evading detection through sleight-of-hand or superior intelligence but by resisting the most fundamental apparatus that makes possible his apprehension. He is always one step ahead of the mind that tries to arrest him."

The approximate two-thirds of Lena's brain that either struggled to stay focused or got lost trying to understand what on earth Tomas was talking about found employment elsewhere. Lena had discovered her first tangent from this conversation through a thought that she often had when talking with – or listening to – Tomas. She always felt the same instinct. It was the instinct to record. At school, if the teacher had ever asked a difficult question or picked on a pupil to compute a taxing sum, Lena wrote the problem down. She wrote down the problem because she knew that, though she probably couldn't solve it in her head, she could, with enough commitment, work it out slowly on paper. She was happy to admit that this reflected poorly on her innate intelligence. She had no illusions about that. But she wanted to try; and to solve the problem with the resources that were available to her meant that she needed more time. But the world of the understanding followed a tight schedule and would not admit a rear-drear candidate. This meant that she held a permanently deferred application to the school of knowledge.

It also meant that, in later life, she collected many unused notepads. Numerous notepads were scattered about her flat; they had all been bought in the white heat of a resolve to make the effort to understand. If someone at the delicatessen had, for example, provided her with an anecdote about the expenses of root canal work, she would stop by the newsagent to buy a pad in which she could research more about dentistry. She once decided to write down every word she didn't know in a pocket-sized notebook which she would carry with her wherever she went. But Lena never remembered the notepad; occasionally, she bought new ones whenever she heard a new word, though she had often forgotten the word she didn't know by the time she found a stationery vendor; and sometimes she forgot the instinct to buy a notepad before she could even forget the word she didn't know. There were too many simple things that distracted Lena, like hot air balloons and small children who walked into lampposts.

Lena was also more interested in the aesthetics of her stationery than their utility. She had bought several faux-leather bound sketch pads and a coffee-coloured jacket for refills. She took these home after purchase and flipped them between her hands, as though she was judging the quality of a fresh fish; she stroked them and left them placed carefully but casually on the edge of the coffee table with a silver ball point pen clipped into the spine. This, if it did not demonstrate the practice of research, gave a confident impression that it had – or might have – once occurred.

Now that Tomas was in free-flow, her fingers itched for pen and paper (or, in one of her more pedestrian corridors of uncensored fantasy, a personal stenographer). She was not, at this stage, interested in a dialogue; she only wanted all the available facts stated plainly and in such a way that she could understand them. And then she wanted a protracted moment in which to consider each fact in the context of the other facts. But Tomas was not like a meal; he did not provide a list of ingredients, a set of simple instructions and a serviceable product. Neither could Lena keep pace with his explanations (or speculations). She would latch onto a single detail, like human sacrifice, and picture pot-bellied men wearing buffalo hide, shaking incense in a consecrated mountain refuge as a young victim lay stretched out on the altar of sacrifice, like a marinated tranche of steak. By the time this image had fully formed in her mind, she would have missed several crucial facts in the assembling case.

And even if she had the opportunity to collate all the information in her own time, she knew tacitly that she would never get around to it. Even with all the time in the world, the extent of the analysis would exhaust her will to understand.

Lena, sitting on the bench, by now not really listening to her uncle, decided that her notepads were a waste of time. She would collect them all together at the next opportunity and give them to an aspiring writer living in penury. He or she would make better use of them, she thought. And by the same logic, she felt a twinge of impatience with her uncle, who surely realised that she was not cut out for this kind of investigative snooping. It all seemed like a roundabout way of asserting a given: that this murder, like so many other things, was something she would never understand.

"You may recall that Henry developed his interpretation by reading through articles from old copies of the local newspaper. In each of these articles, he identified a difference between the meaning of the events for the writer of the article and the meaning it held for Henry (or, at a stage further removed, the *true* meaning of the events). Henry, through a simple comparative study had realised that, if the conclusions of his study were correct, then the interpretations of each writer were in some way wrong. For example, the writer who reported the case of the eastern European girl attributed her death to her involvement in organised crime. It is unlikely that it would have occurred to the writer that she was the victim of a murder that took place over eighty years ago.

'So, as I have already tried to indicate to you, the model of explanation Henry developed radically questions the perspective from which these writers interpreted each set of events. The same applies to us looking back now. It calls into question all perspectives on the events that have taken place at all times.

'But it is interesting with, as it were, this in mind, to look at the way the different disappearances have been interpreted. It is interesting to examine the character and motive of these interpretations. All the interpretations that we know about come from the newspaper. This is reasonable enough as it happens to be one of the most public ways to record information. In these cases, the motive is, I suppose, to make the facts known and then, if possible and in a way that will not incur damage to the newspaper, to put it in some sort of context. More often than not this context is, as we have seen, a widely known issue of the moment, which in the hands of less scrupulous journalists, might take advantage of popular prejudices and perceptions. But in all cases the piece is governed by the accepted practice of the press: their need to communicate clearly, and in an engaging way with their audience. Their facts are structured and calculated for effect. The key information is 'frontloaded' and there is never too much information to lose the attention of the reader. The style is concise, the language spare, clean, functional. So, in this case, though there is not a colourful character shouting his opinion through the page, the production-line reporting is the character that comes through.

'But then these can't be the only interpretations. Each of the victims had a life of sorts; they were known by people and these people would have seen the events in their own way, from their own perspective. The myopathic lady who died in the 1950s might, for example, have had a friend. Perhaps her friend, with a unique knowledge of the victim's life, formed a view that the lady engineered her suicide by drowning herself in the river. Perhaps that friend saw it as a tragic case and concluded that her suicide highlighted a shameful lack of public resources for those who require private care. In this case, the affection for the victim and the personal views about the inadequacies of modern society shine through.

'All of these cases will have been filtered through the investigative processes of the police. They will hold records, statements, evidence collated in a professional way. And they will have studied their evidence to arrive at conclusions. Their job is not governed by telling a story or even keeping the public informed; neither is it an intimate view of the victim. Rather it is a hard-line attempt to look at the facts from a legal perspective, in order to address the question of public justice. It ministers to the needs of the law. Their actions are governed by the grammar of society.

'There must be many interpretations, some official, some private, some opinionated, some reticent, some personally involved with the victims, others who saw it all unfold from a distance; and the irony is that it is these interpretations that stand between the interpreter and the true course of events. Because their interpretation is developed out of the historical context of the interpreter. It reflects who they are and their role in relation to the facts. The newspaper reporter sees discrete bits of information which can be moulded into digestible food for a hungry readership; the friends of the victims perceive each event slanted by associations and facts that public records could not possibly know. All interpretations are built on the foundation of the interpreter's personality, of their background, their assumptions, the unique way they puff up their pillows, comb their hair, cultivate their herb garden, inflect their sentences, take an interest in the small-town politics of the day. But the murder, as I have tried to explain, is broader than any context out of which it might be encountered. It is a fallacy of all those who stumble upon events associated with the murder to assume that it will fit within the scope, the idiosyncrasies or even the duration of their life, their job and their explanatory universe.

'This means that all interpretations are, from the hypothetical perspective of the murder, equally mistaken and equally pointless. It makes them look as ridiculous as a dog chasing its tail.

'So all those people who have, at one time or another, encountered a victim of the whistler are tricked into the assumption that their view of the events amounts to a study of the case in question. This may comprise no more than a few idle thoughts of reflection, or it might take the form of an official police investigation. But the truth of the matter is that the murder they are investigating – and in many cases they do not even know that it is a murder – is really just a mirror reflecting the person who happens to be standing before it. To use a different image, the murder is like a frame in which to portray the onlooker. It throws into relief all the habits of thought, the eccentricities of character, the assorted and eclectic quirks of their life from which, and out of which, they run up against a fragment of the complete story. In short, they are not studying the murder; *it* is a study of *them*."

IV

In the first few months following her move to the town, and in a bid to meet more people, Lena had become involved in some communal activities. She went along to church fetes, jumble fairs and flirted briefly with the WI. She met many people in these few months, mainly women, and mainly older women. Most she had only talked to in passing. One of the few with whom she became friendly was May Hudson. May lived in a semi-detached cottage on the edge of the town. She had grown up as the daughter of the local vicar. Her family had moved to Norfolk in 1954, where her father had taken a post in a different parish. May, who discovered a nostalgia for her childhood in the town, returned in the late 1960s as an art teacher at the local grammar school. Unmarried and now retired, she spent her time painting, reading, and living between tearooms.

Lena had formed a friendship with May because she was intrigued by her. She was not as brittle as some of the other women she had met; she had a whirring, impatient intellect and spoke her mind indifferent to any offence it might cause. Where she managed to alienate some would-be allies, her blunt comments bounced off Lena, who saw this, next to the rough and tumble of kitchen life, as the sign of a robust character.

Lena visited May periodically though not on a regular basis; sometimes, she would do May's shopping and at other times, she would help her with her cooking. She did this not out of charity, but because she was interested in May and enjoyed her company. She liked to listen to May talk about her childhood in the town and she was constantly awed by the library of books she kept in her house, most of which were not literature, but works of psychology, social science and art history. Lena was interested by her friend's attachment to the town. She often said that, even if the Vikings invaded again, she would stand firm. She was, in her own words, 'a local sacrament with creaking joints'.

In late march, Lena, on a whim, baked a plum cake and arranged to deliver it to her 'friend from the past'. She trundled across the town and found May stooped over the waist-high brick wall at the end of her garden. Her hair was basin-cut, and she wore a white cross-patterned dress with frills at the hem. Lena could see immediately that there was something unusually sombre about her; and as they trotted through the first rounds of small talk, it became clear that May was distracted by something.

"Do you want a cup of tea?" asked Lena once inside.

"Never mind about that," replied May shortly. "Can't you see there's something on my mind?"

"Why? What's the matter?"

May looked at Lena sternly, examining her for traces of wayward behaviour.

"Sit down Lena. I want you to sit down. I have something I want to tell you. I can't get it off my mind."

"What is it?"

"It's a story."

"I didn't think you liked stories."

"I don't, and I like this one even less than most."

"What's it about?"

"It's about a man (though I can't say I had ever heard of him). I heard it from my friend Pat, and she heard it from her friend Judith, and as far as I can tell, Judith heard it from one of her friends; for all I know, that friend heard it from somewhere else ... God knows how the whole thing got started! This is the problem with stories."

May folded cautiously and mechanically into one of her armchairs, levering her backside onto the cushion, like a rock climber calculating the most prudent route up the rock face. The inside of May's house showed signs of decay and disrepair: faded florid wallpaper had started to come away from the wall in patches, there were gaps where door handles had once been, and the surfacing in the kitchen had come loose. The décor of the house belonged to a different age; it suggested the presence of a fast-fading energy unable to keep pace with the changes of modern life.

"There was a man in the town not so long ago. He was called Phillip. This man was fat. He was very fat. In fact, he was clinically obese. I don't know what he did in the town or even where he had come from, but he knew almost nobody. There were one or two friends he liked to rely on. And there was even a time when he liked to go out. But that stopped. He lost interest. He lost interest because of one friend in particular.

'When he had first moved to the town, he had formed a close friendship with someone from his workplace – like I say, I don't know where he worked exactly – and they would go out at the weekend. His friend was called Dave Barber or Danny Barber. Or maybe it was Duncan Barber, I don't know (his Christian name began with D). I think Dave was also quite new to the place, and with that much in common, they formed a friendship and a small group of buddies – drinking buddies mainly. They went into one of those dark, undecorated drinking holes on the high street: *The Mitre* or *The Black Swan*, I can't remember which. After about eighteen months, something changed dramatically. Dave Barber got a girlfriend. She worked as a care worker at the nursing home behind the housing estate near Samson Street graveyard. With her arrival, the fat man detected a change in his friendship with Dave.

'The fat man saw, after only a few weeks into Dave's relationship with the girl, that Dave had started to behave in a different way. Where they had once spoken freely in front of each other, the fat man sensed that Dave was keeping secrets. Dave had also become more playful and mocking; in the pub, he would lean back with his arm around his girlfriend. They would laugh and make jokes about other people in the pub, like bar staff or eccentric locals; and they started to make jokes about one woman in particular. This woman, like Phil the fat man, was very overweight. She arrived each evening on a bicycle, which looked like it was about to collapse under the weight of her body. She would sit in the corner of the pub, drinking gin and making sighing noises or tut-tutting noises. The fat woman leaned back on her chair one time, lost her balance and crashed to the floor; her legs knocked over the table at which she was sitting. Peanuts and gin went flying. Dave and his woman could barely contain their laughter.

'From then on Dave and his woman started to make their jokes about the fat woman more public; they were all about her physical appearance and often about sex. Dave said things like: 'Imagine lying on top of that! It would be like trying to balance on top of a beach ball; you would keep rolling off!' And increasingly, when Dave had made these comments, he would turn to his fat friend Phil and say things like: 'Don't you think so, Phil?' or 'Maybe you could have a go, Phil?'

'When Phil looked at the fat woman in the pub, he would notice that sometimes she started talking to herself; she would mutter things under her breath. Her words were inaudible most of the time, but if she were sitting close enough and if she spoke loud enough, they could hear her say things like: 'Two poor days doesn't make a week' and, to herself, 'You lazy bunny; just dial that number!'

'Phil the fat man, for the first time in a long time, began to worry about his size and weight. He started to diet; he read the health and fitness supplements in newspapers. Any programme about weight-loss he watched carefully. He heard one woman on the radio talk about the growing problem of obesity; she said many people could find no sympathy for obese people because at the end of the day, when push comes to shove, it is a simple matter of choice. No-one, she said, is born obese; people choose it! Obesity, she said, is a kind of moral failing. It follows that those who suffer moral failing of this kind should suffer pangs of guilt. And that's why Phil the fat man started to feel guilty about his weight.

'He ate less, he exercised more, but he found that the effort was too great, and that he could not find the motivation, or if he did find the motivation and made the effort, then it made little difference. And when he was defeated by the sheer problem of his own body, he made a heavy-hearted journey to the hog roast.

'It became such a problem for Phil that it became an obsession. He never let it show in public but it preyed upon his mind in private. He could wander around the house or around his office in a daze, thinking about the number of chocolate bars he had eaten or calculating the number of calories he had ingested since his breakfast.

'The frequency with which Phil met up with Dave and his woman lessened as Dave's relationship became more serious; Phil started to think that Dave and his woman didn't want to have anything to do with him because of his weight. These thoughts came to a head one night in the pub. Dave had been talking with his girlfriend and some of their other friends all evening, and Phil had kept quiet. Dave cracked a joke about packing a few more pints into Phil's stomach when Phil turned towards his friends,

"I have let you all down, I know,' he said to them. 'But most of all I have let myself down. I know it is my weight that makes me feel bad about myself. I know that if I lost weight I would feel better about myself. Whenever I have tried to lose weight it has not made any difference. I know I need to try harder. Then, perhaps, I will deserve some respect. I am sorry.'

'Phil stood up and walked from the pub. The phone was ringing when he arrived home. He answered and the voice of a girl with a strong eastern European accent came through loud and clear on the other end of the line. She said she had seen an advert Phil had placed in the town Post Office for a bicycle he was trying to sell. She said she might be interested in buying it, and wondered if she could come around to see it some time. Phil told her that it would be fine and they arranged a time. But then she asked Phil if he lived on his own. Phil told her that he did. She asked him if he was single. Phil said that he was. The girl hiccupped a laugh over the phone and hung up.

'The girl phoned Phil again on the day that she was supposed to meet him. She said something unforeseen had come up, and she would not be able to meet Phil to examine his bicycle. She said she was sorry but she asked if Phil could hold onto the bicycle for her. She asked if they could arrange another time. Phil was in no hurry to sell his bicycle and so he agreed. Once they had agreed on another time, she asked Phil if he was on his own.

"Are you on your own today?' she asked.

"Yes, I live on my own,' he replied.

"But nobody is with you?' said the eastern European girl.

"Nobody. I am on my own,' he replied.

'The girl said:

"How does that grab you? Being on your own, I mean?'

Phil said he was happy on his own.

"You don't find it too lonely?' she asked.

"Sometimes, I get a bit lonely. But I have friends,' he replied.

"They aren't always very friendly though, are they? Your friends, I mean?' she said.

"What makes you say that?' he said.

"I have seen you with them. They aren't always very friendly, are they?' she asked again.

"Not always. But you've got to take the rough with the smooth,' he reasoned.

'There was a pause on the other end of the phone. You have to imagine that it sounded as though the girl was thinking about Phil's logic. Then she said:

"Do you have all your clothes on?'

"Yes,' said Phil, hesitating slightly.

"Do you think I have all my clothes on?' asked the girl mischievously.

"I really have no idea,' said Phil.

"Try to imagine,' she said and hung up.

'Phil received many more phone calls from the girl. She re-arranged their scheduled meeting about the bicycle over and over again. Once they had made the re-arrangement, the girl started to talk personally, playfully and intimately. Phil would have found her a nuisance but for the constant postscript to their conversation. At the end of one phone call she told him that, for each of their previous phone calls, she had phoned him from the same place, seated at the side of her bed, dressed only in her underwear; she said she would be completely naked for all their future phone calls. And she said he was to imagine touching her body as they spoke on the phone. She told him that she loved him, and that he wanted him to seduce her. She said she want to feel him and taste him.

'The longer these conversations went on the more Phil lost touch with his friends. When Duncan asked if Phil wanted to go to the pub after work, Phil started to make excuses. He even mentioned the eastern European girl. He said he had a girlfriend in York with whom he was spending more and more time. That Phil no longer wanted to spend time with Derek and his woman, irritated Derek and he decided to seek out some sort of reconciliation with his old friend. He offered to take him out for a meal. He told Phil that Phil needn't feel so bad about his weight. He told Phil that loads of people were a tad overweight, but there was no reason to get wound up about it. He told Phil that any jokes he had made about Phil's size were just that: harmless fun. Phil enjoyed watching Dave squirm and apologise. And Phil didn't believe for a minute that Dave was sincere. Phil had decided that Dave needed someone to look down on; Dave liked showing off in front of his girlfriend, Phil thought, and now that Phil had retreated and found his own girlfriend, Dave was seething.

'Phil the fat man liked imagining the eastern European girl on the other end of the phone. He wondered what she was really like. She sounded young and sexy. Her voice was a little throaty and corrupted; it walked a fine line between innocence and debauchery. The girl in his mind was a petite nymph, writhing and wriggling on a king size bed full of irrepressible desires as she held the receiver that connected them to her ear.

'The girl decided, out of the blue and after months spent on the phone together, that she would like to meet up with Phil. But, she said she would not see Phil at his apartment. If they were to see each other at all, if they were to meet in the flesh, then Phil would have to make the journey to her place. She gave him an address and they agreed to meet the following night.

'Phil walked across town the following night to the address she had given him. It didn't look like much when he first arrived. I'm not sure where the apartment building was exactly, but it was a very run down building; some of the buildings around it were boarded up. The girl's apartment was on the top floor. Phil buzzed the intercom in the main entrance; nobody answered but someone from the top apartment allowed him access. He walked through into an area decked out like a dilapidated hotel lobby. There were two lifts in the far corner of the ground-floor room; Phil approached them but he soon saw that they were both out of action. He found a stairwell and huffed and puffed his way to the top floor, where he arrived wheezing in a thin sweat. He found the entrance to the apartment without any trouble. He noticed that the door was ajar. He knocked and walked in.

'The room into which he walked was undecorated. He could not believe it. He thought he had come to the wrong place. There was absolutely nothing in the room; there were no tables or chairs, no curtains, carpets or shelving. There was no king-size bed either. And for all he could see, there was no eastern European girl. He called out to the girl but there was no answer. There was only one object in the room. Propped up against the wall on the far side of the room was some sort of contraption constructed from metal bars. It looked like scaffolding from a distance. It was rectangular in shape and it appeared to protrude from the wall. It looked like a cage without any bars. The frame of the contraption was made from metal poles that slotted into each other at the various points of intersection. Hanging from a series of crossbeams that joined the two sides of the contraption at the top was an object that Phil could not quite make out.

'Phil looked around the room suspiciously. He walked over to examine the contraption. The object hanging from the top of it became clearer as he moved closer; it looked like a simple wooden box suspended from the crossbeams of the contraption by smaller metal poles. From the box there extended a number of long and thin, but deadly sharp, needles. They stood still and undisturbed, like sleeping predators. Up close, he could see that there were tracks fixed to the vertical metal poles at the front of the contraption. All the poles were so clean that they sparkled in the light. A large pipe plugged into a socket and fixed the base of the contraption to the wall. He leaned over to peer at this pipe. A choking noise surged from behind the wall, and the pipe and the whole frame of the contraption whirred into life for a few seconds. The pipe, in that small fragment of time, glowed a deep purple. Phil heard the door slam behind him. He spun around.

"Were you looking for something?' said a voice.

'A man in a black suit, white shirt with a close-shave haircut walked from the door to the apartment towards the window. His footsteps sounded hollow on the wooden floor. Phil, for a time, only examined the man. He thought there was something familiar about him.

"I have arranged to meet someone here. I may have the wrong address, though.'

"No you have the right address,' said the man.

"It's just that I was expecting to find someone,' said Phil.

"Yes, I know,' said the man.

"It was a girl actually. Someone I care about deeply,' added Phil.

"Well look a little closer. She may be here,' said the man.

"She gave me this address. It's not what I expected,' Phil explained.

"Look around. Perhaps she is here,' urged the man.

'Phil the fat man withdrew his gaze from the direction of the man, who had now walked over to the window where he leaned casually against the wall, with his hands in his pockets. Phil searched the corners of the room. There were only two other rooms in the apartment, both as uninhabited and spare as the room with the contraption. There were no objects in any of the rooms, so there was no way to distinguish between them except by their shape and size. He could not see the girl anywhere.

"I cannot see her anywhere,' Phil said, returning to the company of the man.

"Perhaps you aren't looking hard enough,' he replied coolly.

"What do you mean? There are three rooms; they are all empty!' Phil said.

"Perhaps I could help you find her,' said the man.

"Have you done something to her?' asked Phil, growing suspicious of the man.

'The man walked over to the contraption pinned against the wall. He stroked one of the metal poles with his hand.

"I think I can help you find your girl. But you will need to trust me. And it involves some risk,' explained the man, looking at the contraption.

"What is this thing?' asked Phil.

"It is a device I created. It could be very useful to you. I think it might help you find your lost love,' said the man.

"How?'

"I will not tell you. I will not tell you anything about the device, only that I believe quite firmly that it will help you. You must trust me,' said the man.

"What is the risk?' asked Phil.

"There is some risk to your physical person. You must be prepared to take some risks to your physical person. In my opinion that is the price you must pay for love. But I will not force you. I have to say, however, that this apartment, these rooms and this device all belong to me, and it is within my rights to expel you coercively if I so choose. I will not expel you from the property but I will ask you to make a choice: either you must ask for the help of this device or you must leave. But, I should add that if you do leave, I think it is fair to say that you will never see or hear from the girl again. You now have a minute in which to decide.'

'Phil thought of the girl's voice in his ear. In no time at all he had decided to stay in the room with the man.

'The man chained Phil's feet to the contraption and secured his hands in two adjustable holes attached to the roof of the device. The man stood back from the machine to ensure that Phil was firmly and safely secured. Phil stood spread-eagled in the centre of the machine, like a pie-eating Vitruvian man.

'Phil looked around the machine, at his fastened hands and at his chained ankles until his gaze fell upon the wooden box and its protruding needles. They were long and crescent-shaped, like the fangs of an absurdly large snake. He watched as at the end of one needle a small drop of the liquid inside the needle accumulated and dropped to the floor. It created a small dark mark on one of the wooden floorboards. The mark evaporated in a puff of smoke after a few seconds.

"What is in the needles?' he asked a little desperately.

"I cannot tell you. Sometimes when others have seen the liquid drop to the wood they have been alarmed. Maybe there is cause for alarm. But not everything that appears alarming is in reality alarming,' said the man, and with that he removed a remote control from his pocket, pushed a button on it, and the same surge of life erupted through the pipe that fixed the contraption to the wall. It fed into the poles in which Phil was now prisoner. Phil saw out of the corner of his eye that the pipe had once again flushed a laser-like purple.

'A loud clicking noise came from above Phil's head. He could see the individual chinks of a chain uncoiling out of another pole. The box to which the needles were fixed moved inch by inch through the first segment of the arc.

"I don't understand,' called out Phil. 'How do I meet the girl if I am tied up like this?'

"It would be best for you, if you remain quiet,' called back the man.

'Phil waited as the chain continued to unravel. It seemed to take an age. Phil's sense of expectancy grew and grew to the point where he became impatient.

"I mean, I don't see the point of this. What's the point of this? How can it work? What does it do? What's in the needles? Why can't you tell me what's in the needles?' he asked the man.

'The man watched in silence.

'Phil, on the point of annoyance, looked up once more at the chain. The last chink dropped out of the pole from which it had emerged and swung loose. Phil caught the sound of something cutting the air swiftly and softly. He turned his head to find the box and needles arriving at the end of their arched journey into his stomach. The impact of the needles, as they stabbed his stomach, was so great that it lifted him off his feet. A small gasp of air escaped his mouth.

'Phil looked peaceful at first with the needles still buried deep in his abdomen. It almost looked like a smile was trying to break out through the expressionless fat in his cheeks. But soon a kind of choleric choking growled in his windpipe. Smoke came out of his mouth, followed closely by a huge dense and engulfing cloud of smoke that swarmed from his throat, through his nostrils and even through his ears! The cloud of smoke clustered around Phil so that he was no longer visible and all that could be heard were the choking noises. When the smoke cleared, it was possible to see thick trails of blood coursing from the sides of his mouth over his face and onto his clothes. Vomit accompanied the blood, expelled from his body by repeated retches and spasms from the gut. This went on until a large pool of blood and vomit had formed around his feet.

'The contraption pulled the needles and box out of Phil's stomach, and moved slowly back through the same arc towards its starting position. A long draught of bloody liquid fell from Phil's mouth as his head flopped forward. He was now altogether lifeless. He looked clumsy and awkward in the machine. His body slumped forward and his hands still hung from the roof of the contraption."

May had watched Lena closely throughout the latter part of her story; she examined her face for reactions and gurning looks of horror. She stood up and walked over to the window without speaking. Lena waited for more or some sort of epilogue, but nothing came.

"So that's the story," said Lena, matter-of-factly.

"Yes, that's the story."

"And your friend told it to you?"

"Yes, it's been playing on my mind, because I can't think ... I mean let's face facts ... it's a ... these things; these kind of stories they skirt across the surface of popular gossip and then they vanish. But, you know, the story is interesting," May continued a little more decisively, "because there is something behind it, I am sure. It is representative. Or figurative in some way. There is a psychological ..."

Her thoughts trailed away.

"...The thing that bothers me isn't the gore; I mean that's just silly," she said with a flourish of bluestocking imperative. "But it means something; that's what bothers me. I am sure if one breaks it down, if one analyses it in the right way, there are hidden meanings. It's one of those myths that are used to express something quite ordinary, I feel sure. A way of *expressing* or *articulating* feelings of violence or ... it has a ..."

"You haven't heard anything like it before?" Lena interrupted.

"No, and that's what I find quite perturbing; there is no frame of reference here."

Lena felt a sudden rush of insanity, and an eerie sense of distance from her elderly friend. She put out the flame before it had a chance to really burn.

"No, I haven't heard anything like it before either," she said firmly.

V

"One of the interesting things, then, about this murder," continued Tomas, "is that it makes a mockery of its investigators. It grants them only a slender slice of the pie. It allows them to look at the murder, or to encounter it, through the stunted orbit of a narrow stretch of time in the complete sequence of events. And naturally the only way in which investigations of the murder can begin to make sense of it is through the strange celestial bodies and luminous sundry moons that comprise this orbit. And this is why all interpretations betray so much of the mind that lies behind them. The criminal investigation betrays the character of the law. The newspaper article betrays the journalist. The views of the grieving relative betray the character of the relative. But though these interpretations might stumble upon or *refract* elements from the events of the murder, they are all inadequate, because none can escape the limited field of vision through which they look at the facts."

Lena could feel sleep rising up inside her. The temperature was just warm enough and the sun was massaging her eyelids shut. She had leaned further back onto the bench, and as Tomas continued to speak, she pulled up her knees, swivelled sideways and propped her back against Tomas' shoulder. Horseradish sauce, leeks and sausages were beginning to fuse unconsciously in her mind. There was nothing ferocious or faintly dangerous about the sound of the river; it moved along in seamless vortices and crosscutting currents.

"On the other hand, the victims so far of this killer, though we are looking at them dimly with strained eyesight through the past, all have one thing in common: they have all suffered some kind of misfortune or disillusionment. They all seem to have been exhausted, ground down, subdued, defeated, or pushed to a point of implosion, as though the killer preys on self-destruction. But perhaps all this means is that the victims are those, through misfortune, or circumstance, or a simple loss of will, who have surrendered their portion of time, their perspective, those who, through a gruelling process of self-mortification, no longer have an appetite for their slice of the pie.

'And perhaps between the investigators and the victims, there is another sort of person. This third character is untroubled by the limitations of their perspective; they are reconciled to it and subsist in the world of their internal quirks and uncoordinated corridors of personal space. They do not guzzle at their slice of the pie, greedy for more. Neither do they renounce it entirely. They are content to nibble."

Tomas stopped talking, as though he had waved goodbye to the last words in his head. He remained seated on the bench, propping up his niece as he stared at the sedges, the willows and the slow motion of the river.

Robert Stewart

The body

I

A man in a sacque suit had taken to exploring Lena's apartment. He would walk out of Lena's bedroom, through the small hallway, over the scattered shoes and the hanging coats that concealed patches in the wallpaper. He read from a broadsheet newspaper printed in small type and with almost no pictures. Lena always saw the newspaper first as he turned into her front room. He would stalk across the room, skilfully avoiding the old obtruding curtain rail which Lena had still not thrown out. He would perch on a chair. He would glance at her and smile.

The man repeated this routine for several weeks. His sudden appearance followed roughly the same sequence of nuanced events; he began his short journey in another room to Lena, climbed through the hallway and into whichever room Lena happened to be lounging, where he parked his posterior. He always entered in the same way, his head buried thoughtfully in the newspaper, and he greeted her with the same walk-in-the-park smile. He was like a fragment of executable code caught in a loop the full potential of which remained unexplored.

The man looked like he might say something – almost as though he was asking permission to say something – whenever he sat down in Lena's company. There was a pining and expectant look in his eyes. Lena could not figure it out. She felt that she was meant to respond to the man in some way, but she could not see how or in what way, or even why.

The man's query came through his smile; his mouth carved upwards into his cheeks, his eyes widened and his eyebrows raised. It was an expression that reminded her of a teacher or a care worker with a condescending manner. When no reply came from Lena, the expression folded into something calm and philosophical, and the man returned to reading his newspaper.

The date of the man's newspaper changed and the headlines changed. There were stories about political turmoil, insurrection and instability throughout scattered parts of the world; there were stories about the political machinations of government; there were stories about industry and the economy; there were advertisements for cigarillos, new model cars and luxurious sanatoria in places like Bridlington and Filey Bay.

The man wore the same or similar clothes all the time; the colour of his shirt changed, though its style was constant. The suit never changed. His hair was always bryllcreemed so that an unctuous sheen came from the smoothed wave over his scalp.

Lena tolerated the man for a long time, in the same way that she might have tolerated an alley cat that came to her for scraps. But everything about the man, from the expression of his face whenever he sat down in her company, to the way he tapped his foot on the ground as he read, suggested that Lena was meant to respond to him in some way or another.

Lena returned one night from an evening shift; after three glasses of wine, she was woozy enough to let her mind run free. A painter and decorator at the bar had told her an unlikely story about a man who had hacked his own ears off just to avoid a nagging wife. Lena hoped she would never drive a man to such extremes. If she did, she tried to envisage what life would be like if she were married to a man with no ears. She thought it would mar the relationship. Lena liked men to have big ears, if possible. She liked flicking ears from behind.

She was still thinking about an earless marriage as she settled down before the television when the man appeared. He found a seat at her table by the window, from where he buried his head in his newspaper.

"What would you think," Lena asked the man, "if your wife cut off her ears?"

The man looked over the top of his paper. He looked pleasantly surprised by the question. He raised his eyebrows first, in an exaggerated and comical way so that it almost made Lena laugh.

"At my most ungenerous, I would have said that it would have heralded no obvious drawback. But, on the other hand, it would have meant that any remonstrance would have fallen, not so much on deaf ears, but on no ears at all, which might have worked to her advantage. In any case, I would have been very surprised if she had ever considered it. Though she is no longer with us. Why do you ask?"

"It was just something I heard. Something I heard ... someone told me in the pub."

"The pub isn't always a crucible for accurate information."

"No, I wasn't sure if I should believe the story, either. I think he may have been pulling my leg. But even so. No ears! It's a weird thought. Why would someone do that?"

"They must have seen an angle."

"Some angle!"

"But I suppose someone must have said that when, for example, Newton advanced his theories about gravity. And how do we think about that now? We take it for granted."

"Are you saying that in the future everyone will cut off their ears?"

"No, no, I wasn't saying that. I was only saying that some ideas, which at first might appear to confound common sense, may be informed by an unforeseen reason which we might on closer consideration acknowledge as a legitimate reason."

"I can't see a legitimate reason for cutting off your own ears."

"But when someone first explained the idea of a steam-propelled engine or the printing press there was, in all probability, someone who could see no reason for it. We are heir to an ever-growing tradition of invention and discovery which constantly challenges many of the assumptions we may hold about the world at any given time. But popular opinion is often, first, obdurate and obscurantist and, second, fickle."

"Yes but even so. I mean. Your ears. How could that work well for you?"

"Self-harm is not unprecedented. Ascetics, hermits, recluses, flagellants all enjoy respect and admiration from some religious communities. They see a reason for it."

"Well what's the idea?"

"Perhaps you should have a one to one with a flagellant. I was only making the point that invention and innovation are, by definition, challenging. I have a strong private interest in the history of innovation. It is my belief that with the advent of modern scientific methodologies we live in an unprecedented age of discovery. Inventions have snowballed since the nineteenth century."

The man explained that the twentieth century had continued a tradition established by the nineteenth: it was a great age for inventions. Across the enlightened world the Eureka moment had struck. Strange noises, smells and cries of joy and frustration had come from reclusive sheds, basements and attics, as those who dared to dream found the materials for their revolutionary idea. He talked about a spirit, an intellectual *joie de vivre*, a belief that anyone with perseverance and a questioning mind might deserve an entry in the encyclopaedia of human endeavour. Such faith in the powers of human industry was contagious, he said. It only took one act of discovery to inspire others.

Great innovations, he said, spawned many lesser inventions. The causal reasoning and mechanistic way of thinking, which had altered learned approaches to knowledge had made possible many other minor inventions which had entered everyday life in ways that 'the masses' barely noticed anymore. The man said he had a personal interest in inventions, and he had even worked on a few of his own.

Patent offices could not keep up with the imagination of the backroom inventor; no sooner had they registered one idea than another idea even more brilliant and even more inventive would come along. There were many examples: Bakelite, jeans, teabags, toilet paper.

"Knowledge these days moves at such a rate, that most of us can barely keep up," he explained. "Soon we will inhabit a world constructed from materials and tools about which we will know very little but upon which we will depend. Knowledge is outgrowing us; there is in the imagination of those that think about these things, a vision of the future in which scientific knowledge grows out of control, in which a beast of our own creation controls and constrains us. I have an interest in science and technology and I can begin to explain this idea, I think. The one thing you will observe is that, as often as not, the people who conceive these world-changing ideas work alone, or at least in small communities. There is a very good reason for this. There are only a select and elite group of people who are capable of understanding their ideas. It requires training and application to even imagine them.

'There is a view that all these discoveries are the building blocks of a complete structure at which we will eventually arrive; in which case all the many discoveries constitute *progress*. But suppose there is, for example, a backroom inventor, like myself, who lives in a remote part of world. In this part of the world, the other inhabitants do not have the same degree of schooling and have an interest only in stories of hula-hula girls and derring-do. This inventor discovers a new drug. In order to discover this drug he has undertaken copious research and performed many exacting calculations which require an above-average intelligence. This drug serves some purpose in his community, and so he begins to produce it and administer it to the community. The inventor, through old age, ill-health or an accident, dies leaving behind him an industry which manufactures his drug but which does not understand the biochemistry of the drug. The *science* is lost. But the *mechanism* created by the science remains. And at that point, in that particular community, the science has transcended the people it serves. Science, you see, will make us kneel in the same way that God once made us kneel. And the fervent scientist, like the edifying preacher, has the full authority of a mysterious truth to vindicate his actions."

"Are you a scientist?" asked Lena.

"I have studied science. But I never had the opportunity like some others. I would have liked to have been a scientist. But perhaps there is still some hope for me. I might be self-taught but some of the best scientists were self-taught. I have a project on the go. I have an invention. Though it is nothing world-changing, I believe that few will understand it in the way that I do. I think it will outperform the intelligence of most, certainly everyone in this part of the world. I have put a lot into it, you see. I have put a lot of my time and the thoughts I have conceived in that time into my invention. Some of those thoughts are so unique – I do not mean original but just unique to me – that I believe few will relate to them."

"What is your invention?"

"It does many things. I am sure that future generations will look back on it and laugh at the materials I have used. Today we build houses from brick or stone; whereas in the past they would have used wood. But I believe that the materials are not that important. It's what I have done with them that really counts. That's where the true spirit of invention lies. The machine I have developed is a fairly crude device. I botched it together by studying different manuals. The real secret of the invention is the elixir it delivers. And that, I am afraid, is so secret and so complex, that I could not possibly divulge it to a stranger."

"I am sure I wouldn't understand anyway. I was pretty rubbish at anything scientific."

Lena toyed with a curl of her hair. She wrapped it around her finger. When she unwound the hair a money spider crawled out and onto her finger. She looked pleased.

"Maybe one day I will be rich," she said, as she let the spider spin a web to the carpet. "Do you think your invention will make you rich?"

"No."

"That's a shame. I thought that was the idea with inventions."

"No, the idea is to make some sort of contribution to knowledge and *then* get rich. But I have no interest in riches."

"But will you still say that when your invention makes you rich and famous?"

"It won't make me rich and famous," said the man irritably.

The alcohol was beginning to take its usual toll on Lena's state of wakefulness. She slumped further into her armchair. She wished she had chosen to sit on her sofa when she had walked into her sitting room, but she could not find the energy to move now. She had started to sink into the warmth of the cushions.

"What did you call it? An elixir? What's that?"

"A potion. A concoction."

"I often made concoctions when I was younger. I would take all the bottles I could find in the house, like alcohol, shampoo, make-up remover, washing-up liquid and mix it all together. I often wondered if it would do anything but I didn't dare drink any of it, so one time I rubbed some on the dog. It didn't do anything. It just made the dog grumpy."

"You would not rub my potion on the dog."

"My father called his mother's gravy magic potion because he said it made him feel special. I don't quite know how she got the taste. She used corn flour, I know. And lots of onions. It was an onion thing, I think."

Lena imagined her grandmother pouring gravy over the border-collie they had kept as a child while her grandfather sharpened a long carving knife and laid out the mint sauce. She always envied cooks who could devise something she could not replicate. It was something about food that had always perplexed her. Looked at objectively, a simple recipe, if the cook observed every teaspoon, every knob of butter and every pinch of salt, ought to produce the same meal each time. It was something she relied upon as a professional. But some cooks had a way of cooking certain dishes that, even if they disclosed the recipe, she could never replicate. In certain dishes the personality of the cook came through. She might be able to cook the dish and cook it with greater professionalism, but she could only find an ersatz flavour of the original personality.

Lena, if she compared the history of cooking to the history of science, realised that scientific inventions were celebrated above culinary inventions. There was a whole culture of learning that had grown up around people like Charles Darwin, Francis Bacon, Galileo, Einstein and Niels Bohr but where were the statues of the person who invented lemon meringue pie? Or lasagne? Why were plaudits and accolades not awarded to the man or woman who had thought of pigs in blankets? In Lena's utopian future institutions would hand out prestigious awards for ground-breaking work conducted in specific areas. There would be the Pulses Medal for Innovative uses of the Kidney Bean. There would be the R.B. Protein award for experimental work with Rump Steak. There would be the Fat-face Commendation for the inclusion of Fruit in Pastry-based Cakes. She thought there would also have to be awards that encouraged good practice, like the Fighting Fit Prize for Salutary uses of Lard.

"My potion requires careful administration and a sound understanding of its properties," said the man.

"Can you drink it?" asked Lena, sinking further into her armchair as her eyelids drooped.

"My potion requires careful administration," the man repeated. "It must access the body and the blood stream in a unique way. It would serve no purpose to swallow the solution."

Lena's eyelids were closed. An image of an old-fashioned east-coast momma baking lemon meringue pies set against the background of an orchard had popped into her mind. She was one of Lena's historical heroes: the mother goddess of one of her favourite sweets.

"But what does your elixir do exactly?" she asked, falling into a sleep.

The man leaned forward; his eyes looked over the sleeping damsel stretched out before him.

"It destroys," he said gently.

II

"I learned recently about the true meaning of the word 'heresy'," said Tomas.

Tomas had invaded Lena's apartment uninvited. He could not even find the common courtesy to knock on her door; the door had been ajar, he said, and so he had just walked in. Lena had been in the bathroom when Tomas had arrived; she walked into her kitchen to find him leaning over the preparation area.

Lena had known from the moment she saw him that he was the bearer of bad news. His face looked drained and all the energy he placed in his everyday thoughts was temporarily defeated.

"The way in which we might use the word heresy today, is actually different from the way it was used in the past. Today, the word seems to have the connotation of 'absolute deviation from the truth'; it implies that faced with two competing visions of truth, one must be correct and the other false; and the one that is false is the heresy. But the word heresy derives from the Greek word *hairesis*, meaning 'choice'. This means that a heresy actually has the connotation of 'choosing to emphasise a particular element of the truth to the exclusion of others', which is a different thing altogether.

'There was a heresy I once read about, mainly because I liked the name. It was called Bogomilism. Bogomilism was a medieval heresy of the tenth century, stemming from the teachings of the Macedonian priest, Bogomil. It argues that the physical world in its entirety is the creation of Satan, that the body, the corporeal world, is irredeemably corrupt and that only the soul proceeds from God. Now, if we read Bogomilism in the context of the true meaning of the word heresy, then Bogomilism must contain a measure of truth. But what is that measure? Here is a doctrine that teaches universal cynicism towards the world, that all motivations informed by the life of the body are categorically corrupt, base, evil, assertions of a necessarily malevolent self. Here is a doctrine that creates an insurmountable gap between time and eternity, duality and unity, between man and God. Here is a doctrine that says the world as we ordinarily know it, is not the *real* world!

'Of course Bogomilism was not unprecedented. It belongs to a much broader and eclectic history of cosmologies that fall under the modern label of 'religious dualism'; Bogomilism influenced the Cathars of southern France and northern Italy and was influenced by strains of Manichaeanism (the 'Religion of Light'!), early Christian Gnosticism, even the broad sweep of Zoroastrianism. These various cults and controversies, despite their differences, have many things in common. And the things they have in common seem to me to derive from a common logic. The thread appears to come from the ancient world where there emerged the idea of a god, given various names and fulfilling various roles in religious practice, seen as malicious, mischief-making and duplicitous. This god comes to be associated with the alluring but destructive life of the physical world, of the body and the senses. Dionysius, for example, the ancient Greek god of wine and revelry, seduces his adherents with intoxication and orgiastic abandonment, driving them into a state of self-destroying ecstasy. These beginnings provide a template for later demonologies that can account for moral evil as the activity of a deceptive deity, which leads to the formulation of two distinct realms: the realm of the body and that of the soul. The world of the body, into which we are born and to which we are naturally drawn by the actions of the deceiver god, contrasts with the purified realm of the soul and the beyond, the preserve and creation of a good creator god.

'This *picture* of the cosmos determines what we can say and know of the cosmos and affects how we act in relation to it. Knowledge or *gnosis* for the Gnostics was not informative or polymathic but esoteric and mysterious. It was based on their cosmogonic mythology, on their account of the cosmos and the origins of evil. It was premised upon the idea of a prelapsarian state, an unconditioned state of unity. You might say that the Gnostics, like most dualists, saw ordinary life as the life of a sailor who, every now and then, peers into the deep and murky depths of an ocean the bottom of which he cannot possibly perceive. For most of the time this sailor is preoccupied with the flotsam and jetsam that float on the surface, but sometimes he is troubled by rumours or opaque visions or occasional glimmers of light from pearls on the ocean bed. Such visions might arouse the curiosity of the sailor but were he to attempt to dive down in search of the hidden secrets of the ocean, it would destroy him. It falls only to a select few, a trained elite or elect ('Cathar' means 'pure one' and 'Bogomil' means 'worthy of God's grace') who serve the fragmented sparks of divine light that they see are trapped in the illusory dross and tedium of the world and which call the human soul to its natural home.

'This, of course, has serious implications for the way a dualist might lead their life and it had serious implications for the reputation they acquired among those in the Orthodox Church for whom their views were anathema. Dualists of one sort or another tend to become anticlerical, iconoclastic and ascetic. The only formal structure of both Bogomilism and the Cathars turned on the idea of a second baptism (referred to in the west as the *consolamentum*), for the elect few who serve the interests of the esoteric knowledge in which they believe. But otherwise it is essentially chaotic; the dualist is like a latter-day anarchist, a subversive voice of dissent who cannot accept the idea that *any* institutional authority has a legitimate voice. And with his devalued view of human institutions, the dualist decries the life and times, the most urgent needs of the body; he becomes an ascetic, starving the body of its 'natural' needs. It is on the far side of this self-overcoming, of this moral 'darkness', that we finally begin to discern the 'light'."

Lena had not paid attention to everything Tomas had said; as usual, she could not follow it all, and she was distracted by her intuition that this potted religious history was only a preamble to a revelation she might understand.

"As far as these heresies are concerned, I think it is important to ask the question: if they choose to emphasise the difference between body and soul, with all the implications it has, what informs this choice? What shapes and conditions this repulsive reflex movement of the mind? And that, from the orthodox way of thinking, from *my* way of thinking if it comes to that, is the hardest part of the story with which to come to terms. The historian might tell us that these heresies are social responses to their time; we might see the Bogomils, the Cathars and the Gnostics as a sort of theoretical reaction of protest against an official institution that has turned corrupt and lost sight of the values in claims to represent. We might see them as outsiders, persecuted minorities disenchanted and disillusioned with the narrow scope of the political institutions of their age. Perhaps their iconoclasm was more forward-looking and idealistic than their dissenters gave them credit? One way or the other, the lonely voices that wander outside the radar of the status quo often have good reason to do so. You will find that some monks, if you scratch the surface of their personal history, had an extreme lifestyle in their former life. The same is probably true of drifters, losers and loners the world over, all of whom might begin to empathise with a dualistic way of thinking. And if we stop there, we can etch out another picture of the world, within the parameters of which we might explain the dualistic picture of the world.

'Suppose there is just one 'god': the god of the physical world. He is warring, thieving, striving, capable of kindly acts and compassion, capable of understanding and innovation, but far from perfect. And among the evidence for his imperfection are the poor, the hungry, acts of injustice, the excluded and politically alienated, and so on. Suppose, for a minute, that you are in some way a victim or an example of this god's imperfection. This might give good ground to think poorly about the god's handywork, and your awareness of a better life might cause you to speculate, even fantasise, about something with a greater degree of perfection, even an alternative sphere or realm of perfection. Here, then, is another genealogy of dualistic thought, based on a more reductive way of thinking. And on this account, there is something tragic about the dualist; the tragedy is simply that the ordinary world has done a negligible day's work; the tragedy is that it has left the latest convert to dualism in a world of illusions. It may be working for some people somewhere but not in that instance; and the lesson to learn, therefore, is that the ordinary world should be improved. So if the god of the physical world pulls his socks up, learns and applies a greater knowledge and understanding, then we are in a position to prevent the 'tragedy' from ever occurring. Dualistic thought is finito!

'But then, on this account, dualism is not a heresy at all! It is a demob-happy psychedelic trip of the imagination! In other words it has got the wrong picture *entirely*. And in the place of words like 'god' or 'gods', 'demon', 'soul', 'light' and 'darkness' we can start using words like 'determinate' and 'discrete', or 'analysis' or 'matrix of explanation'.

'The characteristics of the dualist I find hardest to reconcile to the god of the physical world are his or her asceticism, self-abnegation and iconoclasm. This is for two reasons: these characteristics are, by definition, fundamentally mysterious and difficult – not impossible, I admit! – to explain; and that the dualist sees them, not only as desirable, but as desirable like nothing else is desirable. It is the strange combination of the two that interests me about the dualist. We might be able to explain the 'peripheral' by reference to the 'centre', the 'bad' in terms of the 'good', the 'insane' in terms of the 'sane', but when those placed, for whatever reason, on the periphery have taken a good look around and decided that it is *better* than the centre and *better* than the good and the sane, then it serves as a powerful challenge to everything smoothed over by assumption. You might even be tempted to believe them!"

Tomas pulled out from his sleeve pocket a cut-out page from the local newspaper. He had folded it up small, into eighths. He sandwiched the folded paper between the palms of his hands. Lena could just make out a photograph of a familiar-looking woman standing outside the Wallace Roebuck Hall not more than five minutes' walk from her apartment.

"Perhaps, then, it really is a heresy, meaning that there is perhaps a modicum of truth in the perspective of the dualist. Who knows?! I have never met a self-proclaimed dualist, and while I am sure it would be fascinating, it must also demand a high level of idealism. They must be the ultimate believers, those who have subscribed to belief at the expense of everything. That would be hard to take. They would be so fussy! It would be impossible to even break wind without reflecting upon it as an exertion of some sort of self-aggrandising power! If I had invested strongly in a particular commodity and some hyped-up zealot proclaimed it worthless, I think I would find it irritating. Dualism would bring out the worst in me. It would make me want to smoke cigars and spend my money recklessly. It would make me want to leave my soiled underpants lying in the hallway! But perhaps then I would have created a different sort of heresy! Maybe on a better day I would try to bring to my reckless instinct a degree of understanding. But the dualist is a heretic: he has just one simple and singular judgement. However harmoniously it might strike, he has only one string to his bow!

'It is perhaps easy to correct the dualist's myopia. I cannot believe that he looks at the stuff of things and is not at least tempted to see something richer and more inspiring than his scepticism. We might draw his attention to love, beauty, beer and wine or the simple pleasures of a pork pie and a pickled onion. We might draw his attention to various examples of philanthropy or even – where it exists – of good government. We might muddy his absolute judgement against the world. There are many possibilities.

'And if there are many possibilities, there are the possibilities for different images to explain those possibilities. Perhaps, we are no longer sailors troubled by unfathomable messages from the deep. Perhaps, there are people, or there is a person standing before us. Perhaps they are in a room and the room is dark. We are looking directly at the figure, trying hard to make out the features of their face. There is, from behind the person, a source of light. And the figure turns their face partly towards the light so that some of it is visible, but we are forced to squint in order to make out detail (and even then parts of the face remain in the shade). So in this case, the vision is like a light bleeding around the edges of a partly silhouetted figure."

Tomas unfolded the newspaper cutting. He spread it out on the table before them. Even upside down Lena recognized the photograph. It was the same one that they had used the first time around. The smiling face in the context of the headline looked as disingenuous as everything else she had come to associate with it. It was lying for the camera and, temporarily, it made her think that all camera-smiles were disingenuous. Tomas rotated the paper so that Lena could read it. The headline read:

'Body of Missing Worker Found in River'.

III

Lena had only seen the Terrier once since their night of love. They had spent an afternoon shopping together in Leeds. They mopped up a few mochas and peered through their reflection in shop windows. Something had diffused, however; the Terrier was more guarded. He had pickled a part of his personality for long-term preservation. And since their afternoon together, she had heard nothing from her latest prospect.

She waited like a nervous job applicant. She had tried to contact him; she had left him messages, but he had not replied to any of them. She supposed he was busy organising his cultural exchange or advising wealthy clients whether or not to go double-breasted. Lucinda advised that she should hunt him down and demand explanations. Mark advised that she should give him space. He said she should give him free-reign so that he could sort his male self-esteem out. Mark explained that the Terrier was at this moment like a male lion seeking a place of authority in the pride.

"You've got to let him roam and roar for a while; then he'll come strolling back."

Mark also seized the opportunity to explain that many men in the modern world are alienated from their evolutionary instincts by a 'capitalist logic of repression' in which 'the interests of the subject become subordinate to the financial interests of bourgeois producers'. Mark added that it was possible that the

Terrier suffered from the consequent 'social and psychological schizophrenia between private and public life'. Perhaps, Mark suggested, the Terrier had trouble expressing his true feelings. Lena took notes.

Lena mooched around her flat when she wasn't working. She looked for minor jobs to do: she sellotaped a broken shelf back together, but it soon broke again; she checked her stock of garlic and olive oil; she hunted for toenail clippings underneath the sofa. There was an orange on a plate that had moulded, and which she had resolved to remove several times, but which she managed to postpone at every available opportunity. The skin of the orange had punctured and its sticky and sickly juice had already spread out over the plate.

The man in her flat had developed a habit of surprising her. She would be clearing up some newspapers or crawling around on all fours underneath the table and turn to find the man foraging the middle pages for a daily dose of information. Since their conversation about inventions, the man had formed a new routine. He no longer waited for Lena to initiate the conversation. Lena could be engaged, full-throttle, in an activity, and the voice of the man would take her by surprise.

"Oh by the way," he would say, as he stroked his feet thoughtfully.

"What's that?"

"Do you know how to darn a sock?"

"No."

"It's just that I would ask the wife but you know how it is."

Lena felt like telling him to darn his own sock.

She sensed that the man had treated their last conversation as a gateway through a formal barrier on the far side of which he could adopt a more informal and 'friendly' attitude to her.

"I heard," said the man on another occasion, "that you have a gentleman."

"Where did you hear that?"

"Oh word gets around, you know. I also heard that he is causing you some anxiety. Is that true? Is he causing you some anxiety?"

"It's nothing unusual. Most of my relationships don't work out."

"Now I wonder why that is," said the man.

"I don't know."

Lena thought for a while.

"Maybe men think I don't take them seriously."

"Or maybe they don't take you seriously."

"Why would they do that?"

"Some men aren't very nice."

"They just fancy a fuck, you mean?"

"Some men are like that. Perhaps daughters generally learn from the experience of their mothers."

"My mother died when I was young."

"That was my suggestion. I was trying to play the part of your counsellor."

"My friend thinks it's all to do with Marxism."

"How so?"

"He thinks *everything's* to do with Marxism."

She thought of Mark sitting in his armchair reading an article in the latest issue of the *Socialist Worker* called something like "The Property-based Psychology of Intimate Relations."

"There lived in this town – not so long ago – a boy who had from birth suffered an acute learning disorder and only partial use of one leg (for some time he carried this leg in a brace). Despite this, the boy had a very cheerful temperament and I think it is fair to say that he was universally liked. He slotted into the routine of everyone on the street. He was playful and mischievous. He would let other boys tow him by attaching his leg brace to their bicycles, for example. He often joked that his head was made of wood and invited people to throw things at it just to prove it to them. He once walked into the local constabulary with a dart stuck in his forehead! Some people might say that he was just stupid. But there was something I liked about him."

"Mark the Marxist thinks everyone's stupid. He once called his girlfriend stupid and they argued pretty much non-stop for two weeks. He thinks I am stupid, I am sure."

"Surely not," said the man.

"He's probably right."

"But, in any case, I was not trying to suggest that you are stupid. That was not my point. I only wanted to say that perhaps sometimes you may fall victim to a judgement based, not on objectivity or insight, but on arrogance. Men who just 'fancy a fuck' as you put it, might see you as some sort of plaything for their ego."

"I don't think that's true of Richard; he seemed more, sort of ... scared. But they might, I suppose."

"My wife, in a heated moment, once described the boy I have mentioned as 'a dumb shit of a retard'. She had experienced some trouble with the bank and when she walked out into the street, she saw the boy, she looked at him and she said 'Just look at him! Look at that dumb shit of a retard!' It was not the sort of thing that she would ordinarily say; she was particularly exasperated on that occasion. There are good days and bad days."

The man crossed his legs. He placed a hand on his newspaper, which he had folded in half, and left on the sofa at his side. He stroked one of his many long nails over the surface of the paper so that it created a faint crease down the middle.

"That was my first warning; that was the catalyst that set in motion an entire system of doubt. My wife could be very polite. She could be very considerate. She would even go out of her way to please. When she said it, I remember I looked at the floor and thought for a moment. 'You shouldn't say that,' I said to her. 'What do you care?' she replied somewhat pointedly. That was all we ever said about it.

'I heard her say similar things after that. Not about the boy but about other people. She could make sharp remarks about people; unnecessary remarks motivated by some sort of residual anger that I could never understand and considered from only her perspective. I think my wife was a much cleverer and more sophisticated woman than the town ever gave her credit. She thought the town was provincial and plain. In a different age, she might have made a successful career out of something.

'But, you know, the thing that I always found offensive about my wife's remarks, and about other people who make similar remarks, is that they have such a narrow vision. When the clever person looks at the boy and catalogues him under 'pleasant but insignificant' or 'dumb waste of space' they commit an offence. To my way of thinking it is like staring at only one object in a room full of many objects. They miss something. They fail to see. They barely even scratch the surface. Their remarks are always – or so I find – founded upon a kind of ignorance of the person, which is sometimes ironic when the remark is said with such authority.

'It should have come as no surprise to me, but my wife soon began to treat me in a similar way. When I returned from work one evening, I discovered her passed out on the sofa. She had been drinking. It all started after that. We had an argument the following day about it and it sowed a seed in her mind that I was trying to humiliate her. She said I had been spying on her deliberately. She asked me if I was trying to compile information about her which I might then use against her in some way. 'What is it to you if I get drunk anyway?!' she shouted. I did not say anything to her. I had never intimated any disapproval of her behaviour. I quite understood why she might choose to get drunk. If I had been sitting on that energy, that ambition and – I will use the word again – that anger, I think I would have resorted to alcohol (you have to deal with it in some way!).

'I think, in many ways, the problems that snowballed from that moment were partly my fault. I was never good at confronting my wife. I was never able say what I meant to her face. And I always suffered the belief that if I tried to explain, she would never truly understand. I came to think that she was conditioned not to understand me. She could never see that I never intended her any harm, that I never so much as thought of humiliating her, that it was only ever my hope that the untamed furies in her mind would one day find some sort of constructive expression. But, to show some balance, my wife's error was her blinkered vision; that was the part she played in her own undoing. I tell you now that she was insufferable to live with. I was suffocating in her presence. However conciliatory my response, however open to persuasion I might have been, she found some reason to commence battle. You see, this is the curiosity; I believe she wanted an argument; she looked for reasons to argue with me; she picked on mundane comments or trivial actions and turned them into the most grievous offences. In fashioning the world after her own image, she spied the same anger, the same propensity to judge – and judge harshly – that she saw all the time in herself. And so in the same way that she, like many other people in the town, missed the positive side to the local boy, she misunderstood my real intentions. And what can you do when someone is so committed to a particular view? So resolutely blinkered? When they have wilfully obscured a situation?"

Talking about his wife troubled the man in a way that Lena could not quite unveil. He looked calm on the surface, with his legs crossed, his back propped against the sofa and his newspaper placed at his side, like a gentleman who had taken time out for a morning cup of coffee. But Lena could detect a flickering blue flame of anxiety, kept under control by the safe surroundings of his relaxed appearance.

"My wife developed a habit of interrupting me. Whatever I might be doing, she would find some way to prevent it. Even if I were doing something as simple as reading the paper, she would walk into the room and rip it from my hands. I remember the first time she did it, I objected; I remonstrated with her. Just as she could sense my temper beginning to rise, she grabbed a box of matches and burned the paper before my eyes. She did similar things. If I were boiling the kettle, for example, sometimes she would walk into the kitchen silently and, quite deliberately, she would pick up the kettle and pour its contents down the sink.

'By this stage in our marriage, my overwhelming feeling was regret and, I think, I had lost hope that there might be any kind of future between us. My reserves of energy I channelled into my love of science. My wife would have dearly liked to upstage my interest in this area. I had converted the loft in our house into a small workshop, where I kept all my chemicals and tools. I had a lock fitted and I ensured that there was only one key which I kept in a secret location. Sometimes if I locked my wife out, she would stomp and shout, but most of the time it was a safe place of refuge.

'I had always known that my wife could flirt with other men, but when I first married her, I never imagined this tendency would ever amount to infidelity. But then there were a lot of things I underestimated about her. I noticed that she was staying out more; in the beginning she would ask me if I wanted to go to the pub. The more I retreated to the loft the more she ran off to the pub, more often than not without asking me to join her. Without even telling me. I do not recall that she never came back from the pub or that she ever spent a night outside our house. I can only assume that the pregnancy followed from one of those sordid encounters that you hear about, either in a public lavatory or in a park or down an alley. Something of that sort. The father of her children – I still do not know who it was – soon after he learned of her pregnancy began to spread the rumour, so that it became a sort of open secret that my wife was pregnant by another man. I was, of course, the last to find out.

'I do not recollect that I was upset at the time she told me. Much stronger was the same feeling of regret and of depression, a feeling compounded by the way in which she used my knowledge of her pregnancy. There was no apology; there was no regret on her part. She, I think, saw it as a wonderful weapon thrown her way in the ongoing struggle between us. I do not mean that she used it to her material advantage, but that she saw it as a psychological weapon.

She liked to see the kind of reaction the knowledge of her disloyalty would provoke in me. And when she saw my subdued mood, it often gave her a thrill. I think she wanted to see me defeated in some way; but perhaps I was only in the immediate firing line of a much broader and all-consuming need to defeat and subdue.

'More and more I retreated to the loft where I engaged furiously with the object of my study. I remember writing out notes on the hypothalamus with a sort of manic determination. I could not by this stage quite remove the voice of my wife from my head. Wherever I went she seemed to be there. Even if I went for a walk by myself, I could not escape her and my pace would quicken, my fingers would twitch. It made me forgetful and I lost some of the propriety and order with which I conducted my affairs. This was how she gained access to the loft. I forgot to lock her out. How she knew it was unlocked I will never know because there was no lock on the outside of the door. Perhaps she just tried to open it and, to her surprise, it opened.

'There was a sort of expression of greed on her face when she came into the loft. Her face lit up like a child whose fantasy had come true. She just looked around in near disbelief at all the equipment I owned. At some point between the point at which she first set eyes on the instruments of my research and the point at which she turned her head to look at me, she must have decided which of all my instruments she would destroy first. Without taking her eyes off me, she leaned over her desk and pushed from it a rotating globe which also served as a cabinet for measuring jugs. It had belonged to my father. She then set about the room, kicking things, throwing things, overturning things. The room had filled with a misty vapour and a noxious smell from the chemicals by the time she had finished. I noticed later that she must have spilled some acid on her hand, because when I later removed her body from the house, I noticed that the flesh on the index finger and middle finger of her right hand had deteriorated. It was amazing that she did not do herself more harm.

'I had not really tried to stop her when she destroyed all my instruments of research. I think I stood up and maybe I said a few words in protest. Nothing more. I felt what I can only describe as absolute bankruptcy when she left the room finally. It was eviscerating, and for a while I simply looked at the room in the grip of this hollowed-out feeling. But out of that vacuum there emerged something I had never quite felt before. I had, until that point, always managed to find a perspective from which to assess the way in which my wife behaved and the way in which I thought it best to respond. But, temporarily, I lost that perspective. I could no longer regulate my judgement. It was quite emotional. I became quite emotional. It was a sort of blank rage. I do remember quite clearly my intention and everything that I then did. I picked up a long knife. I walked calmly and coolly down to the kitchen, where I found my wife. She looked at me and she knew immediately what I was about to do. And, for the first time that I could remember, she looked scared. I walked up to her, pinned her neck against the cupboard and stabbed her five times. Like I say, I was quite emotional."

The man uncrossed his legs and leaned forward on the sofa. He rested his arms on the inside of his thighs as he interrogated the coffee table. His shoulders were rounded, like Henry's shoulders, but his face was thin and wiry, like Tomas' face.

"It is strange the way in which events in the external world intrude upon the life of the inner world. The two are connected in ways that often pass unobserved. Throughout the time that led up to my wife's death, I had developed an idea for a particular chemical solution compounded of different drugs. I had often experimented with developing new drugs, and I was always interested to read of the latest developments in the scientific journals to which I persuaded the municipal library to subscribe on my and others' behalf. Drugs, to my understanding, fall into two categories of use: medicinal and recreational. I had always envisaged that the solution I would develop would fall into the former category. My father suffered from a disease which induces a progressive paralysis throughout the body. It affected his gait, his facial expression, even his voice and eventually it killed him. It is my opinion – and it is an opinion corroborated by strong evidence garnered in the scientific community – that this disease is caused by a deficiency of a certain neurotransmitter chemical in the brain which, by acting as an inhibitor, stimulates the central nervous system. It was my aim to create a drug that would address this deficiency. I developed something which – again in my opinion – would, if trialled, produce the desired effect. But I also discovered that the drug would have to be administered in carefully prescribed doses since it has an emetic side-effect. I experimented with large doses of the drug during the troubled period with my wife. I discovered two things: that the drug could produce a prolonged sensation of well-being accompanied by violent vomiting. It was only in the days leading up to my wife's death that I introduced a slow-releasing but particularly powerful toxin into the cocktail, which I knew would be fatal in all cases. It seemed like nothing more than an idea at the time. There was something about the apparent contradiction between the pleasure induced by the drug and its ultimate effect which interested me. So, when I think about it, I do not suppose that the drug is either medicinal or recreational. It belongs in a different category."

Lena stood up. She walked over to the mantelpiece, where she kept a photograph of her parents walking together on the cliffs near Robin Hood's Bay. A thick layer of dust had snowed over several years on the mantelpiece. Her photographs and her candles were tucked in by layer upon layer of dirt.

Lena tried to imagine the look on the man's face after he had stabbed his wife. She envisaged the murder weapon held loosely in his right hand, dripping fresh blood on the kitchen floor. There was, in Lena's mind, no real expression on the face of the man. He was cold. He was distant and objective. He would not scream hysterically or hold his head in his hands. He would destroy the murder weapon, turn his back on his wife and return to his research. He would boil the kettle and have a cup of coffee.

"Would you like a cup of coffee?" she asked.

"Yes please. Black, no sugar."

Lena wandered into the kitchen and put the kettle on to boil. The man, she had noticed, had a way of crossing his legs that reminded her of Tomas. Lena had decided long ago that men who crossed their legs were either homosexual or intellectual. Tomas, she had often thought, could be one or the other or both. She always knew that, if she were in the company of a leg-crosser, she would have to charge her brain and concentrate hard. There was no obvious reason why leg-crossing men should be intellectual or homosexual. Whatever the explanation for it, she always had to fight an urge to reach across and place her hand on the crossed leg, as if to say "It's all right. You don't have to be twitchy with me! I understand!"

Lena toyed with a chopping knife as she waited for the kettle to boil. She made stabbing gestures in the air and ran her finger along the sharp edge of the blade. She pictured the man standing before her after he had stabbed her five times in her womb, the blood flowing over her legs, from her body and from the embryonic life she carried. Her hand reached underneath her sweater and rubbed her stomach searching for a procreative present from within. All she found was a wobble of fat.

"It was a terrible thing that I did," said the man upon Lena's return.

Lena laid out some broken pieces of dark chocolate on a plate along with the coffee.

"Would you like a piece of chocolate?" asked Lena. "I bought you some chocolate."

"Thank you. That's very kind."

"Oh it's nothing. It's just chocolate. I eat too much of it anyway. I'm getting podgy. You eat it. You look like you need it."

Lena watched the man pick up his mug of coffee with one hand and a piece of chocolate with another. He raised his mug to Lena before he sipped from its edge.

"It was you, wasn't it," said Lena. "It was you who murdered all those people."

The man swallowed the hot liquid awkwardly.

"Yes," he replied, resting the mug on his thigh.

IV

The news of Henry's death caused a slight ripple. Lena heard the barman at the Malt Kiln make a comment about it, and two customers in the delicatessen mentioned it as they watched the shop owner slice up some pastrami.

The newspaper reported the story in disbelief: there was no precedent or warning that anyone could find which might have forestalled the tragedy. His parents, who were 'profoundly distraught' by the news, said they had never picked up any signal that Henry had been unhappy. They said they would certainly never have imagined he would harm himself in any way.

The word suicide did not occur once in the article, and yet it was the one word assumed by every sentence.

Tomas leaned back into the sofa, glum and glowering inwardly, as Lena read the article. He crossed his legs and ran his hand over the bristles of hair on his head. He might have looked calm and relaxed in a different context but for the energy that he could not quite restrain, and which found expression in the way he wrapped his fingers on the sofa and crossed and uncrossed his legs again and again.

A woman walking her dog along the bank of the river had discovered the body two days previously. Unlike some of the bodies that had been pulled out of the river over the years, Henry had only travelled a couple of miles downstream to the edge of a village called Thorlby East. There had been a positive identification within twenty four hours. The police had cordoned off his bungalow and were conducting a final search of his belongings for any further evidence. The article did not make any mention of the other people who had disappeared. The article did not even seem to have an awareness of any wider context. It treated the death as a one-off tragedy, a unique event. She could imagine a similar article written in several years' time with the same set of details, the same noncommittal tone, and with the names replaced by new names. The article was just a cast for the rigid construction of the same story retold with different protagonists. It was indifferent to the facts or what they might mean over a broader length of time.

Henry's face in the article – they had used the same photograph, the same silly grin – seemed to smile at her with all the malice of a mischievous world, and confirm truths up to which she would rather not face.

"Why do you think he lied about his name?" Lena asked her uncle. "I don't understand why he did that."

"Who knows," said Tomas. "There was a lot about him that didn't make an awful lot of sense."

Lena had never really thought about changing her name; she had not flagged it up as an option. There were plenty of names that caught her attention and by which she often thought it might be nice to be called. But to actually change her name had always been tacitly off limits. In any case, she was not dissatisfied with her name. She had once had a conversation with a friend in which they had tried to play on their respective monikers. Lena became 'Le', 'Na' and eventually 'Nana', the last of which she shelved hurriedly for fear it might stick.

She thought that he had perhaps changed his name simply because he was bored with it. There wasn't a lot you could do with Andrew ('Drew', 'Andy', 'And', 'Andy pandy'). Though Henry wasn't much better. It was a little like trading in 'Judy' for 'Susan'. She decided this was a bad theory. If he had been bored with his name he would have opted for something like 'Florian', 'Immanuel' or at least something short and punchy like 'Kurt'.

The news of his death was only just starting to break over her; but she did not know how she felt exactly. She had not known him in any real sense. It had just been a passing encounter, like so many others. And most of it she struggled to remember. She did not feel upset or emotional, but drained.

Tomas did not look amused either, as he sat on Lena's sofa while she digested the news about Henry.

"I discovered something else today," he said, trying to read the look on her face.

He reached into his briefcase and from it he pulled out a thin book. He showed her the front cover. On it was an old photograph of the brewery.

"This is a short history of the town. It was written by a local historian, who has written about several of the towns in this region. The book was only published last year, not long before Andrew moved to the town. Here, you can have a look."

Tomas handed her the book. Lena had seen similar books before. She had always thought they would be the historical equivalent to the regional news. She flicked through the first few pages and caught sight of the word 'Ainsty' several times.

"Turn to page ninety four," Tomas instructed.

Lena hesitated for a moment, and then she thumbed through the pages until she found page ninety four. Unlike most of the other pages, the paper on page ninety four was glossy and on it was printed a large black and white reproduction of a photograph from 1891. The photograph showed a clamour around three principal men, all standing on a wooden trailer. Two of the men were wearing a white smock. The other rested his elbow on the prize of white blubber splayed out on the trailer. The whale looked like a dove-white obese child. It did not have enough body room to store its mass, and so large rolls of fat created creases in its skin. The face and expression of the whale was odd; it was puffy like a face beaten into a pulp. Lena looked at the caption. It read:

> 1891, April; *Tom Gregory (featured centre-left), son of Richard Gregory the Baker on St Mary's Street, parades a fledgling sperm whale caught south of the sluice gates at Fenton Field. The whale came to be known affectionately as 'Herbert'.*

Lena stared at the photograph for some time; she read the caption several times and skimmed through some of the text on the page opposite, hoping to catch a more detailed reference to the episode.

"I think in the paragraph that discusses the event, it says that the whale was caught in the tide and that, if it had not been caught, then it would have drowned. Whales have, I believe, been caught out by the tide in many rivers, so this story is not that unusual. I suppose that by the standards of the town it was a pretty unusual event (to the best of my knowledge it has not happened since); but even so, it is not completely out of the ordinary. It created a real stir; allegedly the founder of the brewery – a notoriously crowd-shy businessman – even came out onto the street to see the procession. And it turned Tom Gregory into a minor celebrity. There was, I believe, a short article about the capture of the whale in one of the London newspapers.

'The story is interesting in its own right, but I also find it interesting for the date on which the whale was caught. You will recall that 1891 was the year that the policeman was born. And if you bother to check, you will find that the policeman was also born in April of that year. The whale was caught on the fourteenth of April. The policeman was born the next day.

'It is tempting, I suppose, to think that this might signify something, or that the two events are in some way related. But the capture of whales in rivers is, as I have already said, well documented, and so there is no real reason to think that the dates are anything other than a strange coincidence. But it is an interesting thought nevertheless."

Robert Stewart

The noise

I

Knocking came from the door. Lena's eyeballs rolled in their sockets, like eggs bobbing in boiling water. She had managed to reach her bed this time, and she had managed to half undress. Her duffle coat was screwed up on the floor by a chair in the bedroom, and her trousers hung off the end of the bed. Her hair was still tied back and several buttons on her shirt had broken free. Her eyelids fluttered over the whites of her eyes, and she returned from sleep, red-eyed and pale.

The knocking continued. It was an officious knock unlike the usual knocks at her door. She pulled on her dressing gown and stumbled out of her bedroom into the hallway. The naked light bulb, for which she had failed to find a lampshade ever since her arrival in the flat, was on. She realised she must have left it on when she had returned from the pub the night before. She kicked shoes and umbrellas to one side as she fought towards the front door.

"Lena? Lena are you there? It's Lucinda. I ... we have something for you. Are you awake?"

Lucinda had clearly heard Lena's familiar early-morning movements.

"Don't worry; she will open the door in a minute. She often does this," Lucinda said to someone else on the far side of the door.

Lena pulled the door open, and leaned on it, squinting into the dark daytime of the corridor at the two disturbers of her hungover snooze.

A young man wearing a navy blue uniform and the insignia of the Royal Mail stood next to Lucinda. He carried an electronic device for documenting the receipt of special deliveries. He shoved it in Lena's face, and asked her to sign her name on the screen using the electronic pen.

"Do I write on this?" Lena asked, referring to the device.

"Yes," said the man, letting his impatience show.

"I've never used an electronic pen before," she said.

"You just sign there. Like any other pen."

There was a large parcel next to the postman's feet. It was half a metre in height and about a metre and a half in length. Lena leaned over to look at the package.

"Is that for me?" she asked.

"It better be for you," said the postman, "at least, I'm not carrying it back down the stairs."

Lena stood up straight again.

"Shall I bring it in for you?" he asked. "It's quite heavy."

"Yes please."

Lena and Lucinda looked at the package which the postman left in the centre of Lena's living room. They each stole eyefuls of curiosity from the parcel as they talked.

"He tried to knock at your door but you weren't answering so he came down to leave the parcel with me. I said that I would get you up. I hope you don't mind," said Lucinda.

"No, I don't mind," said Lena, yawning, stretching and folding her arms.

"Was it a long night last night?"

"I wasn't working."

Lena had received a phone call the day before from the Terrier. He had dropped her like a hot potato. It seemed to follow given that she had not heard from him for several weeks; and, in her usual fashion, she had trudged dutifully to the pub where she had got drunk.

"What's the matter?" asked Lena.

"I was just thinking about stuff."

"What sort of stuff?"

"You know, just stuff."

Lena had decided that she needed to go back to school. She needed to find a college that taught elementary coexistence with the opposite sex. She needed an index of warning signs, of clearly marked labels to which she could refer when making judgements about men.

She stretched her legs out on the coffee table and rubbed her right toe against her left foot. The light from the window made her legs look pale and blotchy; it exposed all the natural blemishes that a softer and more flattering light might conceal. She rubbed her eyes and yawned again.

Lucinda looked at the wrapped parcel in the centre of the living room.

"Do you know what it is?" she asked.

"I have an idea but I don't know exactly. Was there a message with it?"

"No. Just the parcel. I wonder who sent it."

Lena wondered if there was someone who wanted to blow her up and if the package contained a bomb. She tried to imagine, for a moment, what it might feel like to have her body parts scattered across the street. With her head on one side of the road she might be able to see her legs on the other. She dismissed the image of her head and Lucinda's head lying on the pavement as they held a conversation about something trivial like make-up remover.

"Well? Are you going to open it?" asked Lucinda.

Lena kneeled down beside the parcel without saying anything and tore strips from the carefully wrapped package. She knew the object as soon as she touched the smoothed grain of varnished wood. Lucinda helped her to strip the object bare. The box was made from treated oak so that the colour of the wood had turned a dark and rich brown that still retained a surface gloss.

"It's a box," said Lucinda. "It looks like a box. Is it a box?"

"It's a box for storing buttons."

Lucinda looked at a large drawer among many drawers. Latches fixed the drawers to the side of the wood. Lucinda unlocked one of the latches and pulled at the drawer. Inside was a collection of buttons in many different shapes, sizes and colours.

"A button box," said Lucinda.

II

In the pub, Lena was seated between her dysfunctional friends from the flat below. Mark, his belly burping over the waistline of his jeans, held a frothy pint of ale as he talked about portrayals of peasantry and 'the earth' in early Russian cinema. Lucinda half-scowled at her beer mat, probably musing wilfully about fancy frocks and Grace Kelly.

Opposite them, sitting on a bar stool, was a young man, who Lena thought, once or twice (perhaps only in passing) had stolen a fleeting glimpse at her. He was tall and well-built, with a straight, girder-strength back and wrestling shoulders that tapered down to a slender waist. He had a mannish certainty congregated in a pack of equally mannish males. Lena looked him over like a freshly exhumed vegetable for quality, firmness and flavour, as she drifted between two states of mind.

The man in the sacque suit had stopped appearing in her flat. He had packed up his wares and was, no doubt, roaming the rooms of a different digs. The noise in her building had also stopped. The battle cries from her close companions in the flat below continued, but they lacked the harmony that the noise had provided; the building and its tenants seemed to have returned to their usual state. She could hear the friendly tinkle in the toilet above and the familiar guffaws of occasional laughter in the flat adjacent.

Though the man was living door-to-door elsewhere, it was fair to say he had made a lasting impression on Lena. For some time, he filled in many of the gaps in her routine; he was the subject of many idle thoughts as she stood waiting by the kettle, or as she gazed out of the window at a man with the use of one arm skilfully lifting the lid of the wheelie bin and tossing in his sack of rubbish in a single uninterrupted operation.

Lena enjoyed Sunday afternoons between her shifts at the restaurant. Sunday was one of her busiest days, but she liked its ambience. Everything became more relaxed. She imagined serious nine-to-five workers reclining in armchairs dressed in vests and pants, reading the Sunday papers over a long and lethargic cup of coffee. Slow, indolent and sleepy music could often be heard coming from other rooms. Even sparrows, house martins and swifts seemed to take things easy, assembling on roof ridges, chimneys, and telephone wires to spend some time catching up.

It was at times like these that she thought about the man. She wondered how he had entered her head; how he had gained access. It had been a steady process. He had gestated from a simple seed into a living organism, explaining himself in fully formed sentences. If she looked back, she could see this slow birth evolving, from the first hints of his presence, from noises that caught her attention in passing. Somehow he had found his way into her flat.

She thought he must have spent some time scoping out the place, like a bank robber recording and studying all the discreet entry points, observing her habits and the points at which she was weakest. This would not have taken much research. She was so wide open she made a commune look repressed. But she was convinced that the man had first entered her flat the same night that she met Henry. It had happened somewhere between the entrance to the building after she had kissed Henry good night and her final inebriated dissolution on the couch. Perhaps he had spoken to her that night. Perhaps he had escorted her to her flat. Perhaps that was why the door had been unlocked. She really couldn't remember.

From this time onwards, his presence had become more and more tangible. And this growing presence had been related in some way to her pratfall investigations. The more she had learned about the murder in the town, about Henry and about the other victims, the more the man approximated to a physical form, until eventually he had appeared in her flat, fully grown, speaking, reading, and breathing.

And in the same way, she wondered if the man had grown up, if only unconsciously, in the mind of many different people in the town. Perhaps he had appeared, here and there, at different times, in different contexts. Perhaps he had many different lives, appearing on public benches admiring the view, smoking a woodbine. If this were possible, then no doubt he had appeared in the early offices of the brewery, grounding out long rhetorical memoranda on a Remington portable typewriter. He would have appeared at fetes, perhaps wearing the clothes of his victims or those who had suffered at his hand. Some people might have noticed. They would make comments such as 'Do you know, Alan Butterworth, the printer, owned a scarf just like that,' and they would let their suspicion surface momentarily before they moved on. He had appeared at car boot sales, selling the possessions of his victims in the early hours of Saturday mornings, giving back to the community the material paraphernalia now deprived of ownership.

Arthur Caulfield had probably attended many church services; he had probably watched many solemn processions dressed in mournful black from a pew at the back of the church. He had probably congregated, head bowed to the ground out of respect for the dead, as his victims were laid to rest in the graveyard, under the crowns of the oak trees close to the popple wells.

The young man buttressing the bar with his rumbling scrum of playmates had definitely cast more than one fleeting glance at her. Lena entertained the possibility that he was checking her out, and, unconsciously, she straightened, pulling in the small of her back so that she could lead from the front. She ran a hand through her hair.

This, to her mind, unequivocal and long-practised signal would at least allow her to test the water. In the interim, she looked at the pack of primates mouthing and drinking in the jungle of bachelorhood. She noticed their collective necks, the cocking and bobbing of Adam's apples, engaged in a squawking anatomical bazaar of activity, like a turkey farm of talking.

III

When she looked at the button box, still unmoved from the same place in her front room, it courted her attention. It was so stolid and assertive that she could not find a place in the room from which she could ignore it. And if she moved it to her bedroom there was not enough room to hide it. She had decided that she would push it into the corner of her living room, and pile newspapers and other bits and pieces on top of it, but, for the moment, she could not muster the energy.

She was also still curious and a little fearful of the button box. She had not yet looked inside any of the small drawers that provided many different entry points to the labyrinth inside. If she were focused on something else, if, for example, she had reached a stumbling point in her attempt to devise a new recipe for the restaurant, her attention turned to the button box; and once it had caught her attention she found it difficult to rediscover her concentration.

She unfastened the latch on one of the smaller drawers one Saturday afternoon when she was struggling to complete an application form. Inside the small drawer were a handful of buttons. She could not see, at first, that the buttons were of a particular type: there was no common colour or size. She tried to pull the drawer out of the button box but it only came out so far. She hunched over the drawer and peered inside to see how it was fixed to the box, but she could not make out its back. She could only get close enough to poke her nose just inside, but there was not enough room to get a proper look. She tried sticking her hand inside. It seemed to go back a long way, the entire distance of which was filled with buttons. If all the drawers contained this many buttons, then the box would testify to generations.

Lena thought she heard something in her front hall. It sounded like someone treading the floorboards. She turned her head, expecting to see a newspaper walk around the doorway from the hall into the lounge. The drawer of the button box closed on her hand, which was still inside it. She let out a stifled squeak of alarm and pulled her hand free. The drawer closed. Lena looked dumb at it. The same sound came from the hallway.

"I'm in here," she said.

She heard the tinny clatter of her letterbox.

Everything was untouched in the hallway. There was no-one in her bedroom or in the kitchen. She opened her front door. The landing area of the first floor was empty. The industrial nervous system of the building breathed a constant flow of air through the walls, and the worn-red carpet led only to a vacant window and a grey skyline.

Her attention was drawn to the staircase, which led up to the second floor. She followed the corner of the wall, behind which the staircase disappeared. She took one step forward and then there was a cough. The cough had the same choking tonality – full of splutter and growl – as the cough she had heard several months ago behind the door on the fourth floor. She stood still; the landing breathed down on her in silence. The cough seemed to throw her naked into a wide open space in which she could only reflect on her vulnerability. She feigned a casual, uncaring sort of walk, and rushed at the staircase.

No-one was on the staircase but there was the footprint of a muddy boot impressed rudely on one of the stairs about two-thirds of the way up. There were no other footprints.

The cough came again, more distant this time, from up just one flight of stairs, but closer to the third floor than the second. Lena pressed on, part scared, part irritated by the sense that something was stringing her along. She walked quickly up the remaining stairs, across the second floor landing and, without giving the source of the cough an opportunity to cough again, she charged up the next lot of stairs. She kept walking until she stood before the door of apartment Sigma. The door was open.

Lena could just make out the pear-shaped bottom of a naked light bulb, sending out a central source of light into an otherwise unpopulated room. The light shone on uncarpeted floorboards and plastered walls partly concealed by occasional strips of wallpaper. There was no more detail on the far side of the doorway: holes remained where there had once been curtain rails, and a perimeter of sharp carpet-grip ran at the foot of the skirting board. There was a supporting wall in the centre of the room, flanked on either side by empty passageways to a room or rooms on the far side of the apartment. The layout of the apartment was unlike any of the other rooms she had visited in the block.

One of the few remaining signs of habitation was a large width of steel fixed very loosely to a circular object, a little like a wheel-lock, obtruding from the wall. Her footsteps echoed throughout the rooms of the apartment as she approached the far wall. The closer she came to the steel object she could see that it looked like a brace or some kind of support for a table; the sheet had been bent at right angles at either end as though it had been made to hug another object.

She peered down at the width of steel. It hung awkwardly in mid-air, dragging down the wall. The circular object to which it was attached had started to come away from the wall, opening a gap. Lena reached out to the width of steel. It felt heavy. She pushed it hard. The two crudely welded objects closed the gap with a loud crash. The steel object swayed about in the air for a while afterwards, which caused something inside the circular object to click. The sound of the click resonated throughout the walls of the apartment and the building like the click of two bones at the joint. The familiar ticking noise, louder and for the first time under control, slapped her around the head and made her teeth go numb.

The door closed behind her. The same dusty voice cleared its throat.

IV

Lena kept herself busy imagining how the man in her apartment might have appeared to other people in the town at different times in its history. Like many things, the man and, what she had come to refer in passing as 'this business of a murder', knelt temporarily before the shadow of her ill-fitting crown and mitre; and, like a child crouched curiously over the edge of a stream stirring up the settled riverbed with insensitive prods, she dallied with it.

Lena was sure that there was a serious way to think about the man in her room; there was a way paved with filed records, testimonies, courtrooms, interviews conducted by jug-jowl men scribbling with biros, business-chic women arranging meetings at which to discuss hearings, due process and scrutinised trails of evidence. But this way was too complicated and bureaucratic. Instead, Lena saw the man popping up in the background of photographs, shopping occasionally from green grocers and queuing up on a Friday night for battered cod and chips. She saw him, aquiline and polite, in the tearooms next to a tray of cinnamon muffins and fat rascals.

Lena spent some time simply walking around the town, looking over it, examining it in ways that she had never stopped to do before. Every object, every corner, every building, every layer of mortar, in the fluorescent tubes of light that formed the brewery brand, shining down, all-powerful, on the town below, had probably seen Arthur Caulfield from one side or the other, at various times in his life; each could tell their own story, or an element within a story – a foil, a twist, a detail, a soliloquy, a joke, an intrigue, a thread.

There were any number of different ways in which Arthur Caulfield might have slithered unnoticed passed the unobservant eyes of the town inhabitants. His appearances would always be appropriate; wherever there was a missing space, wherever there was a vacancy that looked out of character and inconsistent, he would fill the space equipped with the knowledge of his observers' expectations. He had probably been photographed at many different weddings; he would be archived in albums trawled through by grandchildren and relatives who traced over-dressed family and friends with sticky index fingers, querying the identity of the man standing next to their great aunt Penelope.

He would have been the interlocutor of many soused and aggrieved patrons of the ale tap, shuffling between billowing clouds of alcohol to sit down with a pint and a packet of mini cheddars over bitchy conversations about management or the general state of the country. Lena could imagine the kind of internally reflective conversations these scenarios might inspire: pissed partners in crime congratulating each other their rectitude, their disillusionment and their mordant cynicism.

In the mind of hormonal young boys growing up in the late 1950s, their sexual imagination fired by the conical boobs of movie stars and select passages from DH Lawrence, the policeman might appear as the father of a foxy older girl observed voyeuristically through half-parted curtains and peepholes in the wall. He might appear once, maybe twice, glimpsed at summer cricket matches played on the ground owned by the brewery, guarding his daughter carefully.

In Lena's mind, anything seemed possible. Dotty older ladies might hold conversations with the man – in this guise as a polite and distinguished gentleman propping up an increasingly defunct tradition of chivalrous decency – as they queued up at the butcher's shop for brisket.

"After you, madam," he would incline politely in a deep, well-smoked voice.

"Well, that *is* kind. It's not often we see two-colour shoes in the butcher's shop!" the lady would reply, fawning flirtatiously.

Lena was, by this time, grinning dreamily at her own historical inventions. And if she caught herself grinning, the shadow of a shifty look crossed her face, which reflected the momentary guilt she felt, as though the whole world was condemning the desultory and irresponsible chaos of her mind.

She was leaning between the one-sided conversation at her table, her head positioned directly above her glass of wine, and the right side of her face held in the palm of her right hand. Her eyes were like frosted glass; windows only to a mind applying for emigration from empirical fact.

The guy at the bar from whom she thought she had extracted a curious and slightly lusty response, seemed to have lost the wag in his tail. He had cooled and retreated, half-aware of Lena's dissolved awareness (or an awareness at least re-routed via an unmapped cul-de-sac of Lena's mind at the little-known edges of her mental geography). She needed a quick and easy way to reassure him; and so she fixed her eyes in his direction, her head still propped up prominently by her right hand, and stared. If he were even slightly skilled in the arts of cross-room flirting, he ought to understand. Lena avoided subtle techniques. She did not have the equipment to run them efficiently. The man responded; he returned the look with a smile, and threw a joke at his friends, which created a ripple of gravel-chested laughter.

Lena's thoughts about the murder and her reactions to the murderer were like all her thoughts and reactions. They were not planned or constructed to fulfil any prior requirements. She did not actively seek them out or research them; they were the reflex movements of a slaphappy mind dazzled by the beacons of interest in her immediate field of vision. Her thoughts about the murder and her reflections on it were not sensible or considered; they did not follow the long, hard ascent to the truth of police detectives, investigative journalists, and amateur researchers like Henry. Lena's studies, unlike other investigators, were impulsive, incomplete, and easily obscured by the ungovernable leaps and associations of her imagination. She drifted between the facts, musing over one detail in the bath as she chewed on a stray strand of her hair, or moulding the shape of another into a contorted caricature of the truth as she daydreamed about unconventional uses for lemongrass.

This meant that the case went unsolved in Lena's mind. The connections passed unnoticed, the motives undetected, the complete history of the murder remained in fragments, leaving her to stumble from one piece in the puzzle to another, while a theoretical completed account existed beyond her reach, beyond her limited exertions.

This left her in a permanent state of misunderstanding and self-deception. But she was not phased. She could not count the number of times she had been deceived by a situation, or at least the number of times she had misjudged the situation. She was prey to either her credulity or her gullibility. She could not decide which. She was like an innocent picking up shells and pebbles on a beach out of curiosity only to find loitering crabs and creepy crawlies hiding on their underside.

Naivety and carelessness were as constant as a birthmark. She had been conned into buying many spurious items for which she had no use. Despite the fact that she lived in a flat on the second floor of an apartment building, a street hawk had once managed to sell her a gardening fork on the pretext that she might one day own a garden. Lena in reality only liked the process of meeting people, whether they were trying to sell her something or whether they were extracting an eyeful, and this left her prey to any underlying deceit. In the same way she would come home from time to time with a shopping bag full of books with titles like 'Estonian for Business', she would also fall into the trap of misleading individuals who sold her stories about white whales, whistling policemen and careers in journalism. In her more lucid moments, when the true colours of the person or situation shone through, she made a quiet, albeit half-hearted, resolution to think more before she acted.

Tomas was, increasingly, a key player in this process. He was the guardian angel of all her incongruities. Her thoughts could not seem to escape his anticipation; whatever avenue of thought or experience she happened to explore Tomas was always at the end of it, ready to explain her wrong turnings and sense of disorientation. She was an extemporary thought whereas Tomas was the complete idea. Tomas did not abuse this position. He merely poked fun at her.

But Lena bore these imperfections as seamlessly as a stroll in the park. The murder grinned at her like the grotesque mask of an ornate costume. It lampooned her for her failure to produce a study more analytical, more sophisticated, more exact, or *less* absurd. But she responded to these harsh judgements not with fretful consideration and self-reproach but hospitality. She did not lay siege to the murder. She offered it pastoral care and a light lunch.

V

"Were you looking for something?" asked the voice.

It was a man dressed in a black suit and open-neck shirt; the soles of his shoes struck cleanly against the wooden floorboards. He had shaved off his hair to conceal a growing bald patch at the back of his head. He watched Lena closely.

"I thought someone ... I heard something in my apartment."

"You heard something?"

"In my apartment. In the hallway and then on the stairs."

"You heard someone?"

"I heard a cough."

The man coughed.

"Did you hear that cough?" he asked.

"Yes."

"But I wasn't in your apartment. Or on the stairs. I was here. I have been here all the time."

"Is this your apartment? I'm sorry."

"I don't own it."

"It's not furnished."

"The flat is rented by my client. I am his property agent. Though he doesn't live here. He was using it for professional purposes. But his lease has just expired. I have been clearing it of his particulars. Though there wasn't much here. And, as you say, it is a quiet place. Are you sure it wasn't an echo? The cough you heard?"

"I don't think so."

The man leaned back against the windowsill with his hands in his pockets and thought hard about the situation.

"I suppose it's possible that there's someone else in the building with a cough."

"I suppose."

"Have you lived here long? I don't think I have seen you around here."

"I have lived here about a year and a half."

"Oh I'm sorry. I didn't register. Which floor?"

"The first."

Lena waited for the man to say something but he stayed quiet. He rocked against the windowsill.

"So no-one actually lives here then?" she asked.

"No."

"What kind of business did your client do here? If you don't mind my asking."

"He ran a service. It's not well advertised. It's more of a word-of-mouth operation. But he keeps an open door. Anyone is free to stop by."

"Like a counselling service, or something?"

"You could put it that way. Though it is difficult to explain. You see, my client is an inventor. And it is really one of his inventions that attracts his clientele. Sometime ago he invented a machine. This machine he calls the *nous-333* machine. It was attached to the wall, over there."

The man pointed to the width of steel fixed to the circular object.

"It is a complicated device and difficult to understand in abstract. It might be best if I illustrate it by example. Do you mind? Shall I illustrate it by example?"

"Okay."

"Well, for example, there was a young man who visited not so long ago. I do not want to get lost in the long grass of an extensive preamble, but it is worth knowing a little about his background. He had not lived long in the town; and, as I understand it, he did not really know many people here. He had spent some time trying to get to know people, though not very successfully. But, through a set of incidental circumstances, he had learned about a story associated with the town. And he spent a good deal of his spare time researching this story at the municipal library. The story was about a murder. The subject of the story was a policeman who murdered his wife in 1918. And the young man, with an interest in this story, discovered something unusual through his research at the library. He discovered that there were similarities between the details of the murder in 1918 and the details of other people who had disappeared throughout the twentieth century. The policeman who murdered his wife left the body in the river. The disappearances he learned about all resulted in the discovery of a body in the river. The policeman who murdered his wife stabbed her five times in her womb. All the other bodies about which he learned were discovered with similar stab wounds (in some cases matching the exact number of wounds).

'So in the mind of the young man, the story of the historical murder had far-reaching consequences.

He came to think of each disappearance about which he had read as a repetition of the 1918 murder, as though the murder was haunting the town.

'It is fair to say that, for a short while at least, the young man congratulated himself over his investigations. He had, after all, achieved something that, from the evidence available to him, no-one before him had achieved. He had pieced together a series of disparate events and facts from different times and spotted the continuities; and from these continuities, he had worked out a complete story, an interpretation, quite different, quite radical, and quite unprecedented.

'The results of his research turned him temporarily into a true scholar. He had taken the facts as they were known to him by the scruff of the neck and followed the clues, the leads the evidence so that he could assemble a model of explanation, logical and evidence-based.

'But I think the young man must have got carried away with the sheer exhilaration that all the evidence fitted together so neatly. He must have got so carried away that he failed to look close enough at the conclusions he had drawn. No doubt he had collated all the information correctly; no doubt he had thought through its interpretation – but he had not really stopped to think about the sort of impenetrable answers he had reached. By following the detached logic of a scholar, he had concluded that the bodies found in the river over the years were to be explained by a spectral murder; not by accidents, not by suicides, not by anything, in a sense, more plausible.

'And once he had reflected on his research long enough to realise this, it occasioned some anxiety. From a scholar excited by his research, he became a scholar energised by panic that his personal empire of knowledge was crumbling around him. (First comes the ascension to power, then comes the paranoia!) Though the evidence suggested that his theory was correct, the theory itself was utterly illogical and unsound. It simply did not make sense that a murder should re-occur with a series of surrogate victims. Ironically, his studious activity and objective approach to the subject matter had led him to develop a theory that placed him in the ranks of hacks, quacks and the long-distance looks sported by custodians of the paranormal.

'What, he thought, had he done wrong? He had been scrupulous in the scrutiny of his evidence. He had applied his mind as best he could. But at the end of his researches, all he had to show for it was a theory that he might just as easily have borrowed from a book of folklore.

'The young man found that he was fretting so much over this problem that he could not concentrate. He interrupted his Saturday morning stints of research with constant coffee breaks, during which he paced about the landing area outside the reading room of the library. Naturally he only worked himself into more of sweat.

'But late one Saturday morning, just as he was about to pack up for the day, he returned to his work bench after the last of his many breaks to find an envelope bearing his name left prominently between the open pages of the volume he had been studying. For someone who knew next to no-one in the town, this was a shock.

'The young man sat down at his desk, examined the envelope on both sides, and then flipped it open. Inside it he found a note. You have to excuse me as I do not have the details of this note committed to memory, but the gist of it went like this:

'Imagine there are a set of events in which you are involved. You are situated somewhere between the point at which they begin and the point at which they end. You are trying to describe these events from this situation, after they began, for sure, but before everything has happened. And not just before everything has happened – before the events have happened to you.

'The young man read the note twice. He turned over the page to see if anything had been written on the reverse, but there was nothing. He scanned the library for an author referenced and catalogued with the books. A man with sweaty, tousled hair and an indiscriminate fat face was staring at him from the opposite end of the reading bench. The fat man glared, almost angrily, across the bench for a few moments before he stood up, retrieved a plastic bag from underneath his chair and walked out of the reading room. The young man, still holding the note, watched him leave.

'The following Saturday the young man returned to the library carrying with him his usual portfolio of research and the note that he had discovered on the desk the previous week. The first thing he saw when he entered the library at eight o'clock in the morning was the fat man, sitting in the same seat. The young man approached the bench a little apprehensively, settled in his usual chair and unpacked his articles of research. The fat man stood up and walked the length of the bench. He sat down in the seat directly opposite the young man.

'"I thought I should introduce myself," said the fat man. "I saw you here last week. I noticed you were reading."

'"Yes," said the young man, "I am just doing some research."

'The fat man nodded.

'"Yes, I noticed," he said.

'"It's just a hobby really," the young man explained.

'The fat man seemed to ignore the question.

'"I left you a note," he said.

'"Uh huh ..." said the young man. "Yes, I picked up a note. I didn't know who it was from, though."

'"Did you think about what I wrote?" asked the fat man.

'"Yes ... yes, as a matter of fact, I have been thinking about it all week," the young man replied honestly.

"'Did it make sense to you? The note I mean," continued the fat man.

"'I'm not sure ..." said the young man, almost thinking it through out loud.

'The fat man leaned back into his chair.

"'The librarian says that you have been coming here each week for several months now. I guess you must have been researching something big?"

'The young man shrugged his shoulders.

"'I don't know about that. It's a hobby really," he said.

"'Is that all? *Just* a hobby?" said the fat man.

"'Well, what I mean is, I am doing it for my own interest. I'm not a scholar," said the young man.

"'Really! This all seems very scholarly," the fat man remarked, referring to the papers and folders on the desk. "I would say that this is belt and braces scholarship."

"'It doesn't really add up to much," the young man said weakly.

"'Well, you see," said the fat man, "that's where I might be able to help you. That's where my note comes in. You say that you are not a scholar. But perhaps that is how you have approached this case. And a prerequisite of good scholarship is the availability of information. To interpret the information you need to have all the facts at your fingertips. But the findings of your research suggest that you don't. You are trying to describe a set of events – a murder to be precise. Am I right?"

'The young man nodded.

"'Yes," he said.

'"And you have been approaching this as a sort of historical narrative," the fat man continued. "Now you might think that you are the first person to discover this narrative. You might think that you are the first person to have explained it. And the reason you might think that is because no-one before you has pieced everything together in the same way you have. But many other people have talked about, thought about and, in various ways, described parts of this same narrative. They may not have managed to put the information in the broader context of your explanation, but they developed their own, albeit partial, histories. You might think of their take on the events as imperfectly rendered approximations to the real events.

'The problem with these foregoing histories is that they don't recognise the approximate nature of their histories. They see them as true and accurate. They have pulled together details and anecdotal evidence and threaded everything together to make a presentable garment with which to clothe their experience. All these people saw their interpretation in the same way that you see yours: as a safe and objective, a measured, even 'scholarly', view of things that happened. But what they failed to realise – and the same applies to you – is that the narrative is still taking place and that they – and you – are protagonists, witnesses, accomplices, playing a part. Which means their half-baked – sometimes frankly laughable – studies cannot possibly amount to a critical assessment based on objective measures. How is it possible to assess a story that is unfinished? The most that can be said is that they figure as oblique signposts to places in a city they partly comprise. So perhaps the problem you are facing is simply a recognition of the spoils with which you must barter."

"'Well, I certainly don't have a lion's share of the kill," said the young man.

"'That may well be," shrugged the fat man in reply. "But it is essentially a problem of description. You cannot pretend to be something you are not. If you are trying to describe something which is not yet complete, of which you are a part and which will in all probability outlive you, then those parameters limit what you can say; and whatever it is that you *do* say, must recognise those limitations. The 'scholarly' approach you have been following doesn't do that."

"'So what do I do?" asked the young man.

"'You might consider a different approach," replied the fat man. "One that is provisional rather than scholarly, heuristic rather than complete."

'The fat man left these options splayed out on the table, pulled out from the desk and exited the room.

'The young man remained in the library for the rest of the morning, thinking over the things that the fat man had said. He did not have a productive morning, but some of the urgency that had filled him with panic dissipated; he wandered around the reading room, perusing some of the books; he paced in circles in the landing area at the top of the flight of stairs that led to the room. I understand that the young man was now so familiar to some of the library staff that they nodded, and smiled at him, treating him like an innocuous ghost re-enacting the same ritual on a weekly basis.

'The young man felt overloaded with these thoughts, and for the first time in a long time, he began to look at books that were unrelated to his research. He spent some time in the map section recalling the names of capital cities he had learned as a child. He looked in the History section at political biographies, military, cultural, economic and social studies. He discovered several books that took his interest and signed them out so that he might read them during the week.

'One of the books he borrowed from the library was a history of the British royal and merchant navy. Whether he felt jaded after his eight hour day at work, or whether his fixation with the paradoxes of his research caused a fit of mental atrophy, it is difficult to say; he found that when he read the book about the history of the British navy, its details dovetailed with his research. In fact, he discovered that it was *easier* to tell the story by substituting symbols for the key players in the narrative. Where the story he had discovered seemed to lead only to a strange and self-subverting set of dead-ends, he found that by using a more intuitive and familiar narrative, he could tell the story straight, in a way that made sense within the universe of the symbols he used. In this version of the story, the victims he saw as ships sunk in the same year, in the South China Sea, all connected by an elliptical reference to an attacking vessel (the murderer). He found, in this way, that he could use the details from the book to represent the findings of his research that he had struggled to foreclose. The story of the ships was just the kind of imperfect representation for the unfinished history of the murder that the fat man had suggested.

'Quietly confident, the young man returned to the library at the end of the week, where he found the fat man sitting in the same seat, reading a self-help book about romantic relations.

'The young man said he thought he had found a way to describe his research and told the fat man the story of the ships in the South China Sea.

'"Yes," said the fat man, once he had heard the story, "it maps to your findings anyway. So I guess you took on board all the things I told you last time?"

'"Shouldn't I have done?" asked the young man a little incredulously.

'"I am not sure there is really any imperative," replied the fat man. "As I said to you before, it is really a question of description. All descriptions of this murder take place inside the corral of the events they are trying to describe. They are trapped descriptions (or, at least, you could think of them that way). This new version of the story you have told me is different because it recognises, tacitly, the fencing that demarcates the scope of its description. To persist with the metaphor, rather than try to tunnel out, or cut through the fencing that sections-off the corral, it drifts carelessly, whimsically, philosophically, inside it. It has become at ease with these limitations and boundaries, content to play or explore in a lackadaisical fashion. It does not battle with it, trying forlornly to box it into a corner in which it might be controlled and prevented. It is an attitude, or a frame of mind, that would, in coming face-to-face with the murderer, invite him in for a chat and a cup of coffee over a piece of chocolate. It is a perspective reconciled to its nature. It is the perspective of an amateur not a professional. It is predictably inadequate. It is, if you will, like a scientific principle of entropy ..."

'The young man looked pleased.

'"You look pleased with yourself," said the fat man.

'"Sorry," said the young man, a little sheepishly.

'"But, to my way of thinking, a question remains. You have worked out a satisfactory way to describe the murder. But my question is: are you satisfied with it? Because, you see, I cannot believe that someone who has so few personal distractions that he spends every Saturday researching a series of events that would be dismissed as a comical flight of the imagination by the sober-minded majority, would have found the will to understand even this much? What I mean is, if the kind of symbolic explanation we have discussed satisfied you, I am not convinced we would be having this conversation. The truth of the matter is that you want to know how the story of the murder ends, or you would not be here. Am I right?

'The young man gave no answer. He looked a little forlorn.

'The fat man, acting on the momentary indecision, reached across the desk to pick up a pen and a piece of paper. He wrote something on the paper and handed it to the young man.

'"As I have said, the only way you can complete your investigation is once you have played your part and the events of the murder have run their course. If you go to this address," said the fat man referring to the piece of paper on which he had just written, "someone will help you find this perspective. Perhaps you should think it through."

'The fat man stood up once more, gave a valedictory nod to the young man and left the room once again.

'Naturally, the young man spent most of the day thinking about everything the fat man had said, about all the work he had done over the past few months, and about what might lie in store for him at the address scribbled on the piece of paper.

'The address the fat man had noted on the paper was this apartment. He appeared in the doorway over there, as you have just done, at around eleven thirty in the evening," the man in the black suit said, pointing at the open doorway. "Everything looked much as it does now. The rooms were empty and undecorated, as they are now. The unshaded light was on, as it is now. But over here, stood the *nous-333* machine. The young man was dazzled by the room, like a rabbit caught in the headlights of a car. He took small, uncoordinated steps into the room until he came to a halt, unsure of what to do, or what to expect.

'His eyes fell on the *nous-333* machine. The machine is difficult to describe if you haven't seen it. It is framed in a Spartan scaffolding of interconnected poles. Two tracts move in a convex, half-moon trajectory down from the top two sides of the frame towards its centre. At the top of the frame, fastened securely between these tracts by chains, is a box with five arched needles, protruding roughly towards the ground. Manacles are attached to the top and bottom of the machine and its back attaches to the width of steel that you can see before you. It is a strange and menacing thing to catch sight of, and it becomes the focal point of any room it inhabits.

'The young man skirted around the *nous-333* machine, glancing nervously at other areas of the apartment, as though he expected someone to appear. When he reached the machine, he stared up at the long sickle-shaped needles; he could see some liquid inside each of them, and a droplet forming at the sharp end of one. He followed an invisible vertical path to the floorboards beneath the needles. The wood had been corroded and singed where previous drops from the needles had landed. The young man looked sharply and fearfully back at the needles and, with his fingernail, flicked its tip. The drop fell heavily, as though the weight of its chemical properties gave it added velocity. It landed on the wooden floorboard and immediately sizzled into a puff of smoke. The young man took a step backwards.

'"Were you looking for something?" said a voice from behind the young man.

'Standing in the doorway was a man. He was gaunt and suited, even a little dapper. This man is my employer, the inventor I was telling you about.

"'I'm sorry," stammered the young man. "There was no-one here, so I just came in."

"'That's all right," said the inventor. "I like to keep an open door."

'The young man fumbled inside his pockets and produced the piece of paper on which the fat man had scribbled the address of the apartment.

"'I was given this address by a friend. He told me that you might be able to help me. I am … well I am looking for something."

"'Oh really," smiled the inventor, who seemed to approach the conversation with prior knowledge of everything that would be said, "what are you looking for?"

"'I have been doing some research … it's a little difficult to summarise."

"'Well, why don't you give it a go. I am always interested in research projects," the inventor said, trying to put the young man at his ease.

"'Yes, well, as I say, it is a little complicated," the young man took a deep breath. "For the last few months I have been researching a series of disparate events; the disappearance and death of a number of people in the town from the early twentieth century onwards. These disappearances and deaths at first look like they are unconnected, but they have a number of things in common."

"'Oh really," said the inventor, who looked a little puzzled by the young man.

"'Yes, you see, in 1918 a policemen in this town murdered his wife," the young man rattled on. "He stabbed her in the womb after he learned that she was pregnant by another man, and then he disposed of the body in the river. All these other disappearances that I have read about all end up in the same way: the body is found in the river with abdominal stab wounds. So, you see, it is as though the murder is repeating itself."

"'It sounds like an unlikely story to me," said the inventor, frowning slightly.

"'Yes, I know, but the pattern is uncanny," the young man said a little pathetically.

"'So how do you think I can help you?" asked the inventor.

'The young man stared directly at the inventor; his arms went limp at his sides.

"'I want to know what happened," he said.

"'It sounds like you think you know already," replied the inventor.

'The young man continued to stare at the inventor.

"'I was told you would be able to help me," he said.

"'Well," the inventor sighed, "maybe I can help you. But there is one thing I should make quite clear from the start. This isn't going to be easy. In fact it is dangerous. Are you prepared to accept those dangers? I cannot really say any more about them, but they are quite real. So you must consider them."

'The inventor eyed the young man for a moment.

"'I will give you a minute to think it over. If you decide you want to accept my help, then I will help you. If not, I will ask you to leave and never return. Okay?"

'The young man nodded his head.

'The young man did not even pretend to think the matter through. He remained fixed to the spot, staring intently at the inventor until the minute had elapsed.

'"Yes, I could see that you would stay from the beginning," said the inventor. "Now I will help you."

'The inventor led the young man to the *nous-333* machine. He guided him so that the young man stood inside the frame of the machine, and then fastened his ankles and his wrists to the manacles at the top and bottom of the machine, so that the young man stood, somewhat inelegantly, spread-eagled in its centre.

'"There," said the inventor, "now we are ready to begin."

'The young man looked a little confused. His eyes flicked between the details of the machine and the inventor, who was now walking away from the machine towards the window, where I am standing. He felt frantic and panicked, the same way he had felt when he first thought about the findings of his research.

'The machine, though inert, seemed to hug him and enfold him. He gazed blankly at the needles poised for action. They were assembled before him orderly and correct, like a firing squad. He counted them: one, two, three, four, five! And then he looked at the tracts running down from the topmost corners of the frame into the centre, a pre-laid path pointing directly towards his stomach. The needles, and their direction, galvanised his mind and he looked desperately at the inventor, now leaning back against the window frame. The inventor's left arm was extended towards the machine, and in his hand, he held a device like a remote control.

"'Perhaps," said the inventor, "you are already beginning to understand."

'The inventor pushed a button on the device in his hand and the machine jerked into life. The sound of chains moving over sprockets came from somewhere behind the young man, and the machine lurched back and forth against the wall, creating a jolting click like a grandfather clock.

'The young man looked between the box, its needles and the tracts leading towards his stomach. Out of the corner of his eye, he saw a chain fall loose, swinging through the air. The lurching, clicking and banging stopped. The box and the needles suddenly moved serenely and silently, directed through the tracts. The young man watched the needles move in their arched route through the air until they plunged all the way into his lower torso."

Lena took two steps back from the man in the black suit as he continued to tell the story. She looked at the man, and then at the width of steel at which the man was staring maniacally, stirred up by the ecstatic focus of his narrative.

"The young man looked happy at first, as though he was collapsing into the embrace of the machine.

He could not breathe to say anything more. The impact of the needles had winded him; a faint smile seemed to linger about his face, until his eyes began to dilate. A purple hue engulfed the white of his eyes, and his eyeballs started to increase in size; they crept out from their sockets, at such a rate that they soon knocked off his glasses. His eyebrows were raised to their utmost, his entire forehead looked fit to burst, and blood was pouring from his nose when the steam burst out from his eye sockets. His body went into a spasm and he retched repeated samples of blood and vomit onto the floor. The steam continued to whistle out of his unnaturally expanded head!

'It all took no longer than five minutes, at the end of which he hung dead, his body slumped forward, still in the grip of the machine."

Lena could take no more. She bowed her head to the ground, turned her back on the man in the black suit, and ran from the room.

VI

The Terrier had appeared at Lena's front door not long after his last phone call. His appearance and the tone and timbre of his voice had been guilty with a sense of unfinished business. He had not changed his mind, he explained. He did not think the two of them had much 'space in which to grow'. They were like two plants trying to grow in one pot. He said he was sorry he had been so blunt when they had last spoken. He did not, at the time, have things clear in his mind. But in the intervening period he had found time to think about their relationship. He had mulled over it from many different angles, and he said that he could not escape the feeling – it was an 'emotional thing', he said – that something was not quite right between them.

He had said all this in Lena's kitchen over a cup of coffee, like a creative executive sorting out a project. Lena held her cup of coffee between the palms of her hands and watched the Terrier closely as he delivered his explanation and apology. She caught the first chunk of everything he said, but she found later that she could not remember the rest of it. She had found interest in his eyebrows; it was something she had not noticed before, but the hair of his eyebrows had grown in an odd way so that there was no single direction or apparent groom. They had grown thin and interwoven, like a dying hedge in a land of famine. She guessed that he had, sometime in the past, had cause to shave them off.

By the time she had exhausted her interest in his eyebrows, the Terrier had delivered his explanation in full. He looked relieved once he had finished speaking, as though the meaning and sincerity he had put into the occasion atoned for previous sins and formed a mature pact of reconciliation between the two of them.

It was not until later that she took on board his sober message. A fresh wave of introspection followed. She listed ways in which she could be improved. She attached it to the fridge so that each day it would remind her of how she might sculpt and refine her character. The first item on the list read 'Don't get fat ankles!"

She didn't feel any resentment towards the Terrier; she was, from experience, inured to rejection. Whenever it happened, she sprinkled herself in momentary sadness.

Rejection was not something on which to dwell. She could not see the point; and in the same way the Morris dance of her mind locked arms with objects of momentary interest that soon faded from view, her darker, deflating experiences soon acceded to something new and full of promise. Sometimes she even seemed to demonstrate the act of forgetting as the events occurred.

Mark, nibbling occasionally from a packet of nuts, was now expostulating on 'the nominalist logic that underlies the moral emptiness of modern Britain'. Lucinda looked like a kettle about to reach boiling point. She leaned forward, sitting on her hands, trying to restrain herself from socking her nearest and dearest in the mouth just to shut him up. Lena made a mental note of the word 'nominalist'.

She had never really understood the frisson of violence that kept her two closest friends in cohabitation. She hardly ever understood any of the percolated Marxism that Mark talked; and she never quite grasped the anger it provoked in Lucinda. She knew that Lucinda found Mark condescending, and Mark would often seem to be talking down to her. But Lena thought that this was just Mark's instrument of self-expression. She knew that if Mark suffered a personality change, started deferring to the views of others and placing his hand on the knees of his dialogising partners to demonstrate his understanding and open-mindedness, Lucinda would take out an advert in a singles column for an obstinate, pig-headed bore with detailed knowledge of left-Hegelian German social and political thought. Lucinda was always at her most effervescent and charismatic when charging down the, always implicit, suggestion of her ignorance.

Mark had once or twice (and usually on the back foot) let a patronising remark ricochet in Lena's direction, but it never bothered her. Lena rarely became animated. Few things annoyed her; and she did not have the self-possession to act on it if it did. She treated cutting jibes and careerist caustics in the same way. After spending some time in Lena's company, one woman said to her "I suppose it's easy to be loose-tongued if you can't expect much from yourself." Lena, who at first did not recognise the venom in the words, just laughed and said "Yes, I know."

The murderer was disappearing into the low-lying mist across the vale of her memory. If she thought about it, he was not so different from all the other men she had known. Like all the others, he had entered her world with the same curious amusement, getting to know her until they were comfortable enough to sit opposite each other as he unveiled the predicaments and problems from his past. Lena ordinarily listened attentively to these personal histories – sometimes with interest, at other times with perfunctory expectation – hoping that she might find an avenue to intimacy.

But, though Arthur Caulfield had followed the customary pattern of her relationship with other men, he was clearly different. Setting aside the fact that she did not find policemen very attractive – much less ones with a history of homicide – she was aware that they had a different kind of relationship. His preternatural but gentle and unobtrusive infiltration of her life was not bedroom-bound. She thought of him more as a supervisory reminder, a missionary from an obscure memory she had long-since forgotten. He appeared like an official, descending from the higher echelons of power to stop by for an informal chat just to see how things were ticking over.

Like all the other men she had known, he was now retreating into the memories from which he had emerged. He had toyed with her and turned his attention elsewhere. In total, his involvement in Lena's life was like an idiosyncratic incarnation borne out through the familiar rituals of her life. He had taken the familiar pattern of a momentary fling and summary departure, but treated it as an opportunity to test her reaction to the paradoxes he represented. Through this familiar idiom he had delivered his unfamiliar communiqué. This was the visible form his invisible nature assumed. Perhaps unsurprisingly, Lena sat as comfortably with the lawless figure before her as she did with anyone else, faintly aware of, but not quite grasping, the strangeness of the situation.

The end of her brief relationship with the man in her apartment, like her failed relations with the Terrier and other men, did not slow the metabolic motor show of her appetite. She might take temporary refuge in a drink and solicit sympathy over a counter of cooked meats, garlic-stuffed olives and chimichangas, but a chance encounter in a bar could provoke a glassy sideways glance across the room, a little like the look a cat gives to a field mouse who naively assumes a right to roam. It was this look that was now in her eyes as she skilfully kept her distance from the projectile splutter of chewed peanuts alighted on the hot air of dialectical materialism.

The boy at the bar had kept his cool. There was no over-excitement in his eyes, but neither did he feign an arrogant distance. He kept in touch with his friends' conversation, monitoring it to ensure he could respond as and when required, and yet remained one step removed. He languished against the bar so that he was available to any potential distraction. He snatched glimpses at Lena's table, surreptitiously so as not to be appear over eager, but nevertheless asserting an uncomplicated male interest.

Lena, who felt an uncontrollable urge to use her tongue, started poking it into her glass of wine, like a demented child trying to scrape the bottom of an ice cream tub. Luckily, the boy at the bar didn't notice.

"So what, you think I am being stupid?" Lucinda interrupted.

Lena inhaled accidentally and sucked up a spurt of wine through her airways, which caused a fit of coughing.

"People wear commercialisation like a crucifix. Some people even regress to the mean of a recognisable brand in the way they look – literally. 'Beauty' requires a small investment and a minimal attention to detail – high cheekbones …"

"Oh for fuck's sake, people are what they are."

"People are the society that comprises them."

"Mr Mark says you are the society that comprises you!"

"I'm trying to have a debate … can we not just have a discussion?"

"I'm not interested in your discussion…"

"… you don't think that talking about this …"

"…so it's not a discussion at all …"

"…'reason', 'rational debate' …"

"…it's just you …"

" … should play a part in a mature citizen's life?"

"… it's *your* opinion."

Lena was trying hard not to develop hiccups by taking deep breaths. She switched her attention between the boy at the bar and the argument that was becoming increasingly audible and high-pitched. Its cause had escaped her; but she was concerned it might bring bad publicity to her immediate campaign.

"It's funny," she said, like a crocodile of nuns strolling across the no-man's-land between two armies, "but I remember when I was at school, I liked all the kids that were called stupid. Which is weird. Because, I mean, it's meant to be offensive, isn't it? But the stupid kids were often the most fun. They weren't as complicated. "

Mark fell silent, but looked slightly annoyed; his look suggested that Lena had missed the point, or that this argument would hardly wash with a disenchanted underclass. He suppressed his thoughts, aware that Lena's infrequent contributions to his arguments with Lucinda introduced an area of neutrality on which he could not mortar the opposition.

Lena, feeling slightly smug, nestled back into her seat. She had the sense that the couple, who greeted her interruption of their domestic fracas with polite silence, wanted her to steer the mood in a different direction.

"D'you want another drink?" she said eventually.

She climbed out reluctantly from her cosy corner, leaving her denim jacket in her place (she was protective of comfortable seating and didn't like bar stools).

She swayed across to the bar, taking a studied route towards the boy with whom she had exchanged looks of mutual discovery. He ran his hand through his hair and laughed thoughtlessly at a joke, trying hard to conceal interest in her interrogative approach.

Walking towards the boy at the bar, she thought again about her brush with serial murder, about the calm composure of the killer she had allowed to wander freely around the rooms of her flat. She thought again about the resemblance of her relationship with the murderer to her relationship with all the other men she had known. Had he, she thought, flashed across the firmament of her life in order to tell her something? Had he transposed her hackneyed routines into a signal? Of all the men she had known, he was the most unusual. In one way or another, he had sought her company actively. In one way or another, she had been introduced to him; she had been told about his background, about his history, and equipped with this disquieting and disorienting knowledge, she had found herself in a room with him, striking up a conversation.

At the time, she had not thought much of it; but the events were, as always, catching up with her. She was only just beginning to realise how odd and incongruous their meeting had been.

It made her question her sense of judgement (which was already paying rent on its place in the interrogator's spotlight). It was almost certain that she had not behaved in an appropriate way. There was probably a code for private behaviour with spectral murderers that she had contravened. These was probably a perspective – which she had not grasped – from which it all made sense, and in accordance with which she should have responded to the man. But even now, with the benefit of hindsight, she could not fathom it. So, as she approached the bar determined to free her mind of distractions, she decided that her haphazard approach would have to make do. Murderers probably took tea not coffee. But that was in the past.

She stood at the bar next to the boy she had been eyeing. He had placed himself at an available distance from his friends. She glanced sideways at him and he smiled a little awkwardly, conscious that a conversation might be about to take place but unsure of what it might comprise.

Lena, as she waited for the barman to poor her drinks, noticed a crane fly ascend a joist between the bar and the racks of glasses overhead. It danced over the polished veneer and onto the shoulder of the boy standing next to her, from where it sailed up to his neck, treading delicately over a large mole partly concealed by the collar of his shirt. The boy brushed it away with a wave of his hand.

Lena had heard the urban myth that crane flies contain enough venom to contest the life of a human but that, almost cruelly, their fangs are not big enough to deliver it. She wondered if, in the future course of evolution, they might overcome this problem by growing to monster size. In the future, crane flies might haunt the attics of country houses, pirouetting over the floorboards and insulation, and playing havoc with the damp course, emerging occasionally to strike fear into an already complacent human population.

She imagined a behemoth specimen climbing furtively up the back of the boy next to her as they approached a flirtatious conversation. She imagined its head appearing over his shoulder, its mouth slathered in drool, as it dropped a greedy mandible to sink its teeth into the pimpled bullseye on his neck.

She noticed that the boy was half-watching her with a look of restrained alarm.

"Have you ever been bitten on your mole?" she asked innocently, wondering faintly how it might taste.

The boy's mouth opened as he tried to unfurl the sense of the question.

www.ingramcontent.com/pod-product-compliance
Lightning Source LLC
LaVergne TN
LVHW011805060526
838200LV00053B/3672